FIGHTER'S FRENEMY

A. RIVERS

Leo

I grit my teeth as the throb of a bass rattles the nightclub floor. Parties are not my scene. Especially not alcohol-fueled messes like this one. I don't have the patience for this crap, but unfortunately, I have to be here. It's the official after-party for my first professional fight since I shifted from City Fight Center to Crown MMA Gym. I lean against the bar, watching a mass of people writhe on the dance floor. Once upon a time, I'd have been in the thick of it, but I've been involved in the MMA circuit for long enough that fights don't have the same hype they used to. I'm certainly glad my new coach, Seth Isles, worked so hard to get me back in the cage, but I wish all I had to do was win and go home. As it is, my being absent would set tongues wagging. Many people still wonder whether I was complicit in the cheating operation my previous coach and fellow fighters were arrested for.

I wasn't.

Did it surprise me when I found out? Hell no. There are some seriously sketchy people in this business. But I hadn't heard a whisper about it until the police showed up during a training session and started cuffing people.

My eye twitches. My opponent got a good shot in and I've got a hell of a shiner. It'll be worse come morning. If I'd been able to slink back home, I'd have already iced it, but for now, I'm the dude who has to do what he's told and go where his manager wants him to.

Voices to the side catch my attention, the words "drugs," "cheater," and "fat skank" passing through the general noise and pricking my psyche. Straightening, I seek out the offending parties. I level my gaze on the backs of three guys who are facing a woman. I can't see who she is from here, but they've obviously cornered her.

"What in the actual fuck makes you think you can show your ugly face tonight?" one of the men demands.

My jaw grinds. Whoever she is, no woman deserves to be spoken to like that.

"Is there a problem here?" I snap, shoving my way over to them.

All three men spin around, and when I spot their victim for the first time, I nearly roll my eyes.

Camile Hayes. I should have known.

Her wide blue eyes land on me, silently begging to be rescued. Her full pink lips tremble as though she's on the verge of tears, and she hugs herself, emphasizing the way her tits nearly spill out the top of her dress. I swallow past an instantaneous gut-punch of lust. Yeah, Camile is sexy, with thick curves and an ass that's practically pleading for a man's hand to grip it, but she's a princess who doesn't think for herself. She lives in the shadow of her twin brother, Karson, one of the fighters who was recently arrested, and seems to be dependent on him for her confidence and sense of self.

"You." Their leader's eyes narrow. "You're as bad as her. Probably in on it. Fucking cheats."

Oh fuck no. He did not just say that. My jaw locks, and I shove up the sleeves of my button-down shirt, revealing tattooed forearms. "Look, I already beat the hell out of one guy tonight, and I'd rather not do it again. Don't go around saying shit you know nothing about. Leave the poor girl alone and pick on someone who can fight back."

One of the guy's friends steps toward me as though he wants to take a shot, but the leader stops him with a gesture.

"Fine." He holds up his hands. "She's all yours." He sends her a scathing look. "She's probably been passed around by half the men here anyway."

My fists curl tighter, but I resist the urge to plant one in his face. That's the last thing I need right now. When they've disappeared into the crowd, I turn to Camile. "Go home, Cami. Get your beauty sleep. There's nothing for you here."

To my surprise, temper sparks in her eyes. "You don't get to decide that," she snaps, dropping her arms from her waist and advancing on me. This close, I catch a hint of a subtle fragrance that makes me want to lick her until I find the source of it. "I'm sick and tired of men thinking they know what's best for me."

My jaw drops. I've never heard Camile string more than a couple of words together, and certainly nothing as assertive as this. It shocks me. Especially given how she reacted to those bullies.

Raising her chin, she pivots, then sashays away, heading in a direction that isn't toward the exit. I stare after her. What the hell was that? Is there more to the princess than meets the eye?

And why do I want to follow her and find out?

I'm sick and tired of people with penises trying to run my life. I head to the ladies' room, shut myself in a cubicle, and rest my forehead against the door. I don't even pause to think about hygiene; that's how angry I am. Finally, I mustered the guts to do something for *me*, rather than play the role I've been pushed into as Karson Hayes's twin sister, and look what happens. Another interfering male tries to cockblock phase one of my plan.

"Ugh!" I growl aloud, not even caring someone might overhear. I hate myself for getting all fluttery over Leo Delaney even more than I hate him for basically patting me on the head and telling me to shoo. The Goliath-sized blond, who looks more like a surfer on steroids than one of the world's best MMA fighters, has always made me weak-kneed and stolen my capacity for rational thought. But why does he have to look so damn heroic marching into the thick of a nasty situation like some avenging angel come to save me?

Well, not *me* per se. I saw his expression when he realized who he'd stepped up to bat for. Leo Delaney has no patience for Camile Hayes. I'm not sure what I ever did to him considering we've hardly talked, but I could tell he thought I'd waltzed into trouble without a thought in my silly little head. I can't even be bitter about it because it's not as though I've given him much reason to think otherwise. Whenever he's around, I withdraw into my shell and become a stammering, blushing mess.

Not tonight, though.

Perhaps it's all the emotion I've been bottling up seeking a safe outlet, but I couldn't just stand there and take his disdain without speaking my mind. I hadn't been brave enough to tell those bullies off—perhaps because I didn't know them and couldn't be sure how they'd react—but I know Leo well enough to know he'd never hurt me if I let loose a little. Not physically, at least. His friends haven't nicknamed him "Priest" for no reason. It's a better fit than his fight name, "The Lion." While I might not always appreciate his judgmental attitude, I have to agree every bone in his body is honorable.

Closing my eyes, I sigh. He did look awfully sexy with those tattoos winding around his forearms and that tousled golden hair. Even the bruising around his eye couldn't detract from his hotness. It just made him look more like a Viking warrior.

I wish he'd pillage me.

No, Cami. I straighten and give myself a pep talk.

You can do this. Ignore him. You've been managing for years now. Get back out there and tick off Item #1 on The List.

I retrieve my phone from my purse and navigate to the document where I saved the list of things I've always wanted to do but missed out on because Karson undermined my confidence or made me feel foolish for even contemplating them. I set my jaw. I've always looked up to my brother, even if he's a bit arrogant, but now I feel like my blinders have been ripped off and I can see him for what he is: a hypocrite and a cheat. The antithesis of Leo Delaney, and the kind of man I'm ashamed to have given up so much for.

I scan the list.

1. Have a mind-blowing kiss.

2. Get a tattoo.

3. Make a friend.

4. Go ziplining.

5. Pitch my designs to a clothing line.

I return the phone to my purse and grab my lipstick, then leave the cubicle and use the mirror to reapply it. I have a habit of gnawing all the color off my lip when I'm anxious, so they're pretty much bare.

Tonight doesn't have to be a total loss. I came here to kiss Tony, and I intend to see it through. The sexy Italian-American fighter isn't the man I'd most like to kiss—Leo holds that position—but he's a flirt and, unlike Leo, he's actually shown interest in me. Given he's a playboy, I figure he knows how to kiss a woman. I place the lipstick in my purse, check my reflection one last time, and walk back into the noisy nightclub.

The base pounds through my body as I search for Tony. Eventually, I spot him and groan. It seems my would-be kisser has already found another playmate for the night. He's locked at the lips and hips with a curvy brunette who has angel wings tattooed on her back. Seeing the couple together doesn't hurt me. I'm not emotionally invested in Tony. It's just frustrating because I really want someone to kiss the hell out of me. I've been kissed before, but nothing earth-shattering. Not like what they write love songs about. I want the whole experience, and if not for my altercation with those men, and the following interaction with Leo, I might have been the one swaying with Tony on the dance floor.

I turn away and head for the exit, brushing off the hands of a man who tries to pull me into a dance. I may want to be kissed, but I'm not desperate. I have a plan. I've chosen Tony because he's perfect for the job. I'll just have to try again tomorrow. As I slip through the exit and into the cooler night air, I mutter to myself about men who think they know what's best for me. Story of my goddamn life.

2

I wake feeling more refreshed than I'd like. I've had a lifetime of being quiet, sensible Cami, who lives in the shadow of Karson Hayes. Last night, I'd hoped for more. I wanted to do something for me. Something that would shock the hell out of my twin brother and make him give me that disapproving look that always stopped me in the past.

It won't stop me any longer.

I didn't get my adventure yesterday, so I'll just have to chase it today. Tony is hosting an afternoon party at his place for people associated with his new gym, Crown MMA, to debrief. I know he won't turn me away if I show up, even though I don't technically have an invitation. He's too kind for that. Of course, if I go to the party, there's a chance I'll run into Leo again, but I've let fear dictate too much of my life already. No matter how nervous I am about the possibility of seeing him, I won't let it hold me back.

I get out of bed, make breakfast, and spend the morning working on my designs. I'm employed by a boutique for plus-size women, but my greatest passion is the designs I make in my own time. I have dozens of different styles sketched out, but I've never been brave enough to show anyone. Not even Karson or my parents. My brother has always been the talented one, the famous one, the good-looking one. Design is the only thing I have that's just mine, and if one of them laughed or told me I wasn't good enough, I don't think I'd recover.

But I *am* good. I know it. Or at least, I'm decent enough not to be laughed out the door if I pitch my designs to a clothing company. I just need to work up the nerve to do it. Sharing my designs terrifies me, hence why it's the last thing on my list. I'll have to build up the confidence for it.

After fixing a burrito for lunch, I shower and start primping. I choose a gorgeous pink lipstick and pair it with a dress of the same color that drapes over my shoulders, plunges at the cleavage, and gently caresses my curves as it falls to my knees. It's one of my favorites. I designed it myself but had someone else make it, since sewing isn't my strong point. I can get by in a pinch, but artistic vision is more my thing than the nitty-gritty of stitching and adding buttons or zips.

I dust on a little blush, apply mascara, curl my hair, and smile in the mirror. Perhaps I won't ever look like a model, but I'm pretty enough for men who like their girls on the bigger side. I check the time and decide it's late enough for the party to be in full swing. Thankfully, most people shouldn't notice when I turn up.

I drive to Tony's home, a modern building in a wealthy area of town with big glass windows and a terrace overlooking a sprawling lawn. He makes good money, although Karson makes more. Or at least, he used to. This arrest has the potential to destroy his career. I park down the street because the roadside is clogged with shiny new vehicles, and make my way down. I feel self-conscious strolling up his front path by myself. Several people I don't recognize look at me strangely. Across the lawn, I lock eyes with Lena LaFontaine, Karson's ex, who is standing with three other women. I've seen two of them at fight events before—a stunning black woman and an athletic blonde with a dangerous scowl—but the third, a pregnant brunette, isn't familiar. I hold Lena's gaze, sucking in a breath as I wait to see whether she'll make a fuss about my presence. I didn't spend much time with her while she dated Karson, and I'm not sure why they broke up, but my newly cynical side tells me he probably mistreated her. I offer her a small smile, and her icy blue eyes narrow, but then she lifts one shoulder and looks away, dismissing me. I relax. I can handle a casual dismissal. Perhaps this will be okay after all.

"Cami!"

I turn at the sound of my name. Tony is making his way toward me, smiling widely. When he reaches me, he bends to kiss my cheek. His lips are warm as they ghost over my skin, but no tingles erupt. I don't feel the urge to swoon.

Damn.

"It's good to see you, *bellissima*." The corners of his dark eyes crinkle, and a lock of hair hangs free from the tie that's holding the rest of it at the nape of his neck. "It's been too long."

"Hi, Tony." I return his smile and remind myself of my mission. "Good win last night."

He beams. "You were there?"

"Aren't I always?"

He laughs. "True." He takes my hand, but I don't read into it because he's just a touchy person. "Come on.

Let's find you a drink and catch up. I want to hear all about what you've been doing since I left City Fight Center."

A little more of the tension eases from my shoulders. Everything is going well. I can do this. I follow Tony and accept the glass of wine he offers. "Thank you."

"No problem." He leads me to a quieter spot where we can hear each other over the hum of conversation. "I'm glad you came. I've missed seeing your pretty face."

Nerves fizzle in my gut, and sweat beads on my forehead. Now is the moment. I need to flirt back. "Not as much as I've missed seeing yours."

Ugh, Cami, could you be any more cliche?

But Tony laughs, his eyes widening with surprise. He cocks his head questioningly, and I give a subtle nod to indicate that yes, this time I'm willing to flirt. I've always ignored his attempts in the past because I knew he wasn't serious, and honestly, I worried what Karson would say if he found out. He'd probably have made a snarky comment about how I was embarrassing him and making a fool of myself over a man who's way out of my league.

Too bad. Karson isn't here today, and he can suck it.

Tony wraps an arm around my waist and winks. "Tell me more about how much you missed me."

Leo

"I appreciate everything you've done for us," I tell my coach, Seth, as we stand side by side on the terrace overlooking Tony's front lawn. "We'd never have bounced back so fast after the scandal if not for you."

Many people still think poorly of the five of us who defected from City Fight Center in favor of Crown

MMA after things went to shit, but we're recovering way better than we would have without Iron-Shin Seth Isles throwing his weight behind us.

He shrugs. "It's good for me to have you guys here. Builds up our reputation."

I manage to swallow down a remark about how our reputation isn't something most people would want these days. Instead, I say, "Ashlin looks healthy."

His lips lift in a slight smile. Seth isn't an effusive guy, but he's crazy about his pregnant fiancé—who also happens to be his ex-wife. "The pregnancy is going well."

"And the wedding plans?"

He grunts. "Coming along okay, but I just want everything to hurry the fuck up so I can get my ring on her finger again."

I chuckle. "Isn't it already there?"

"The engagement ring," he grumbles. "Not the wedding ring."

"You're such a caveman."

He gives me a look. "You just wait. One of these days, you're going to meet a woman who fucks you up on the inside, and then you won't be laughing."

I gulp because I'm afraid it's true, except it's more likely I'll fuck up any woman unlucky enough to fall for me than the other way around. I'm too much like my father, who was a superstar on the MMA circuit long before me, and who used the fame and fortune to cheat on my mom over and over again while she stayed quiet like the obedient wife she is. When I finally caught him in the act and confronted him, he'd rolled his eyes and said I'd understand one day because I was so much like him that I was bound to do the exact same thing. I couldn't even argue. People had been comparing me to him all my life. One sports reporter even went so far as to call me a carbon copy.

But I'm determined to be different. A better man. Back when I told Mom what I'd seen, I expected her to leave him, but despite how it hurt her, she stayed. When I asked why, she said it didn't mean he loved her any less. I left his gym the next day and moved to City Fight Center. I couldn't stay around to watch them cycle through the same crap over and over. Now, we don't talk much anymore.

"Earth to Leo," Seth says. "You in there?"

"Huh?" I snap to attention. "Yeah. Sorry about that."

"No worries." He searches my face as though trying to read my mind. I let him, knowing he won't see anything I don't want him to. My poker face can withstand even his scrutiny. "Ashlin was waving. I'm going to check on her. You coming?"

I shake my head. "I'm going to stay up here a while longer. I like the quiet."

He nods and claps me on the shoulder, then leaves. I rest my arms on the railing and watch the people assembled below. I scan them, looking for my four City Fight Center buddies: Enya, Tony, Oman, and Vic. I spot Enya talking to Harley, Seth's sister. Vic and Oman are playing cards around a picnic table. But where's Tony? I search the group and finally find him with his arm around a blonde—not the woman I saw him with last night. I stare harder. The girl he's canoodling with has a lush figure and the prettiest pink lips I've ever seen.

It's Camile Hayes. *Again.*

She tilts her face toward him and I growl. The way she's pouting, she's practically inviting a kiss. Doesn't she know Tony isn't a good bet for her? She isn't the kind of girl to hook up and move on, which is all she'll get from him.

Damn, I'm going to have to step in and stop her from getting her feelings hurt. I stalk away from the terrace and hurry down to the lawn. Someone says my name but I ignore them, too focused on getting to Camile.

"Hey, Priest," Tony says as I stop in front of them.

"Tony. Can I borrow Cami for a moment?"

He looks quizzically between us. "Sure." He caresses the side of her cheek. I want to grab his fucking finger and snap it. Doesn't he know she's not the kind of girl he can play with? "I'll see you soon, *bellissima?*"

"Of course. I'll only be a few minutes." Lasers dart out of her eyes with enough power to fry me on the spot. My stomach buzzes. There's so much more to this girl than I ever gave her credit for. I place a hand on her upper arm and instantly realize my mistake. Her skin is smoother and softer than anything I've ever felt. I snatch my hand back and gesture for her to go around the corner of the house, out of sight. She rolls her eyes but does it.

"What do you want?" she demands.

I pinch the bridge of my nose. "I want to know why the hell you're hanging out with fighters. Karson is sidelined for a year, so why are you here?"

She folds her arms under her breasts, and I can't help but steal a peek at them. Those luscious tits look like they'd be more than a handful, and based on the way she's built, they're all natural. Fuck, she's gorgeous.

"Have you ever considered that maybe I enjoy watching fights?" she asks, her tone suggesting I'm a dumbass. "Or that I'm here because I have friends in these circles? Not everything I do is because of my brother."

"Oh." I deflate, beginning to feel like a dick. She's always struck me as such a gentle soul that I thought she wouldn't like violence, but I shouldn't have made assumptions. It also should have occurred to me that after spending years around fighters, she might have friends among our ranks. I suppose I've rarely seen her with anyone other than Karson, but it's not as if she just vanished whenever he wasn't around. She must have built relationships. "Okay, but what are you doing with Tony? Surely you know he's not a one-woman kind of man."

Her eyes become squinty. She's pretty fucking cute when she's mad—not that I dare say it. "I want a mind-blowing kiss, and I think he's the guy for the job."

My jaw drops. "You... what?"

She smirks. "You heard me, Mr. Judgey. I don't care if he's not a one-woman man. All I want is a kiss that rocks my world, and rumor has it, Tony knows what he's doing."

Blood rushes in my ears. I can't believe what I'm hearing. An image flashes into my head of Tony and Camile wrapped in an embrace. My brain short circuits. For some reason I don't want to examine too closely, I can't stand the idea of them together. But if all she wants is a kiss, then there's an easy solution.

I'll kiss her.

I grab her by the shoulders, groaning at the feel of her warm body against mine as I haul her close. Then, before she can do more than gasp, my mouth is on hers. She stiffens for a moment but doesn't resist. I shut my eyes and soak up the reality of holding her in my arms. It's so much better than I could have imagined. She's all soft curves and silky skin. She smells edible, and after only a moment's hesitation, her body molds to mine. A whimper sounds in the back of her throat, her lips part, and I finally get a taste of her.

Savage need tears through my body. She's so fucking sweet. Like watermelon and sunlight. I pull her closer and plunder her mouth. What was supposed to be a brief kiss has taken a turn. The ground seems to fall out from beneath my feet, and I'm drowning in an ocean of desire. She dominates my senses. I can't get enough of her.

My cock jumps to life, eager to join the party, and a sliver of sanity returns. I haven't had sex in a long time, and I can't start with her. I stumble away, gasping for breath.

I can't do this. She's related to one of the men responsible for my career veering sharply off course. Not to mention the fact I've just been telling myself she's the kind of woman you keep—and I'm not looking for that. No matter how tempting she is.

"There." I force the word past lips that don't want to work. "You've had your kiss. If that's all you came for, I think it's time for you to go."

3

Wait, what?

I shake my fuzzy head. I'd thought Leo had become so overwhelmed by passion that he'd had to kiss me, but it sounds like he's just trying to get rid of me by giving me what he thinks I want. My lower lip wobbles and I latch my teeth onto it before he can notice. The last thing I need is to let him see he's hurt me. But did he really not feel what I did? That kiss meant something, and now he's trying to tell me it was a tool in his cruel arsenal?

I straighten my back and pull myself together. It doesn't matter what Leo says or does or why he seems to dislike me so much. All that matters is keeping my dignity—something he's made nearly impossible.

Nearly.

With more sass than I feel, I toss my curled hair over my shoulder and cock my head. "I'm not going anywhere. I still haven't had the mind-blowing kiss I came for."

His jaw drops. *Good.* I don't wait around to see what

he'll say next. Instead, I hurry around the side of the house and back to the party, blinking away tears.

"Hey." Tony's brow furrows with concern as I reach him. "Are you okay?"

"Fine." I sniff.

He tucks me under his arm and looks back the way I came, where Leo is emerging from around the corner. "Did he say something to you?"

I sigh. "I don't want to talk about it, but thanks for worrying. I'm okay. I just need a moment."

He smiles kindly down at me. "You got it, *bellissima*. Take all the moments you need."

I stay with Tony for another few minutes, but it's obvious I've lost my will to flirt, and he doesn't try to make any moves. He just engages me in conversation as though I'm not latched on to his side like some kind of parasitic insect. When I've recovered enough to move past the hurt and embarrassment, I say goodbye. Tony kisses me on the cheek, and once again, I feel absolutely nothing. I'm beginning to think that asshole Leo Delaney is the only one who makes me giddy and fluttery.

"Take care, Cami," Tony murmurs. "Don't be a stranger."

I try to smile, but it's more of a grimace. "I won't. See you around."

I wander back to my car, get into the driver's seat, and rest my forehead against the steering wheel. Then I growl, letting out all the frustration bottled inside me. Damn Leo Delaney. Damn him, damn him, damn him. I hate his stupid, jerkish face. Even if it's very good-looking.

Unfortunately—or perhaps fortunately, depending on my point of view—he *did* tick off #1 on my list.

Whether or not I wanted to admit it to him at the time, that kiss was the best I've ever had.

I start the car and force myself to focus on the road. As I drive home, I think about the second item on my list: *Get a tattoo*. I've always wanted one. A lot of the girls in this crowd have them, and I've always thought they look badass. In some cases, even beautiful. But Karson badmouths tattoos on women. He says they're ugly and I shouldn't do anything to make myself less appealing since men are hardly knocking down my door anyway. But now? Screw him. He's a cheat and a liar. I want a tattoo and I'm going to get one. I've even drawn up the design. Now, I just need to find someone to put it on me.

I park in my apartment building's underground lot and hurry up the stairs. Taking the stairs is a habit I picked up in an effort to shed a few pounds after Karson spent years telling me I'm too fat. But I like the burn in my legs, even if I've decided I don't care about the extra weight. That weight is part of me, and when he's not around to make derogatory comments, I like myself just fine. I smile as I march upward. My brother has opinions about everything, and now that I can see clearly, I'm never going to let him dictate my actions again. Twin or not, he doesn't get any say in my life. As I summit the stairs and start along the corridor, my phone rings. I check the screen and groan. It's my mother.

I raise the phone to my ear. "Hello, Mom."

"Camile. So good to hear your voice. Are you sick?"

I frown. "Uh, no."

"Have you been run off your feet because you finally decided to get a worthwhile job?"

I wince as I slot the key into my lock. My parents don't think much of the stylist at a plus-size clothing boutique gig. The only reason they helped me financially to study for my diploma in fashion design is because I agreed to also train as a paralegal at Mom's law firm. I think they expected me to get excited by courtroom drama and go back to college to become a lawyer, but that's never been my thing. When I left at the end of my second year, as we'd initially discussed, they were outraged—even though I'd fulfilled our agreement to a T.

"No, I'm still working at Curves."

"So if you're not busy or unwell, would you care to explain why it's been over a month since any of us saw you?"

And there it is. The guilt trip. Her specialty. I step inside and shut the door with more force than is needed.

"I told you. What Karson did is wrong. All you guys can talk about is how unfair it is that he has to endure a year-long suspension. It's his own fault. Until he's willing to take responsibility for his actions, I won't sit around and listen to you disparage good people just to try to make him feel better."

"But Cami." She tries her "I'm so reasonable" tone. "He needs your support. This is a difficult time for him. The police are pressing charges for the possession of cocaine."

I roll my eyes as I flop onto the sofa. "Then maybe he shouldn't have had cocaine in his possession, and he wouldn't be having this problem."

Mom makes a sound of frustration. "I've never known you to be so uncaring. You've always supported him before."

"I'm sorry if I'm unsympathetic about the fact my twin brother is a drug cheat." I end the call and switch off my phone so she can't call back. Satisfaction rolls through me, followed by a twinge of guilt. I should have been more polite. She is my mother, after all.

No, Cami. You deserve to be treated well. She may be your parent, but she only wants you when you're useful.

Why do relationships have to be so complicated?

Leo

I land blow after devastating blow on the boxing bag, using far more force than is wise considering I only fought a couple days ago. But I've never been one to shy away from the gym, not even when I'm tired and sore. I like to get right back in the thick of it. I pivot and kick, then throw a right overhand punch—my favorite way to knock out an opponent. While I don't take joy from hurting people, there's something satisfying about winning via knockout. When it comes down to points, there's a degree of subjectiveness that pisses me off.

"Tone it down." At the sound of a voice, I turn and find Seth watching me impassively. "You need to give your body time to recover."

I grimace because I know better than to behave this way, but I've been tied in knots since yesterday.

I kissed Camile Hayes. And it was fucking amazing.

Then I turned around and acted like a dick. But in yet another strange turn of events, she gave me sass right back. I really admired her in that moment, and I don't like finding things to admire about Camile because I didn't think she was the kind of woman who had admirable traits. She keeps challenging my perception of her, and I wish she'd just stay in the box I've kept her in all these years.

"Sorry. I'll ease up."

He nods. "Good. Perhaps Tony could take you through some pad work."

"I'll ask." I force a grin as Seth walks away even though I'd rather not be stuck in close proximity to Tony. I haven't spoken to him since he had his arm around Camile. When I'd seen them like that, I'd wanted to physically tear her away from him. It was for that very reason I've stayed away. I had no right to act like a possessive asshole. Camile and I shared one kiss, fueled as much by anger as lust. She clearly didn't enjoy it as much as I did, so I need to back the hell off and leave her alone. Unfortunately, even with a few angry jack-off sessions, I can't get her out of my head. Her lips haunted me all night, and everywhere I go, her scent seems to follow me. I know I'm imagining it because I showered twice, but I could swear I still smell it.

It means nothing.

"Uh, Leo?" A hand appears in front of my face. "Dude, are you okay?"

It's Tony. I jerk in shock. He's standing a few feet away, but I failed to notice him approach.

"Sorry, I'm in my own world."

"I'll say." His brow crinkles. "You were out of it." He holds up a set of focus mitts. "Seth said to go through some combinations. You up for that?"

"Yeah. Thanks, man." I bump my gloves against his mitts and we take up positions opposite each other.

"Jab, cross," he instructs. An image of him and Camile flicks through my mind, and I smash my fists into the mitt harder than intended. He doesn't flinch. "Sixty percent power."

I repeat the motion with less oomph and manage not to demand to know what his plans are with a certain luscious blonde.

Almost as though he reads my mind, Tony asks,

"What happened with Cami yesterday? You dragged her off and then sent her back in tears."

"She wasn't crying," I snap.

"No," he agrees. "But she wasn't far off." He shifts the mitts to his belly. "Knee." I thrust it at him, and he catches it easily. "The other one." He edges backward as I move forward, throwing one knee and then the other. "So, you're not gonna tell me?"

"Nothing to tell."

He raises a brow. "She was in a weird mood yesterday, and you're in a weird mood today. Seems like more than nothing to me."

"Fine." I push kick one of the pads when he gestures for me to do so. "We kissed, and now I can't get her out of my fucking mind."

A laugh booms from his chest. "Wait, you have the hots for sweet Cami? I didn't see that coming." He stops for a moment and a strange expression flits over his face before he doubles over. "Wait. You kissed her, and she nearly cried? Your kiss is why she had the sad puppy eyes?"

Honestly, can I just kick this idiot?

"You about done?"

He holds up a hand to gesture for me to wait a minute while he belts out another round of laughter. I glance over my shoulder, noticing a few curious stares. Tony straightens, panting. "Okay, I'm good." His face is red, and he's smirking. "But seriously, what did you do to the poor girl?"

My neck hunches into my shoulders and I look away, recalling the callous remark I made afterward. I'd acted like a jerk, and I wasn't proud of myself. "I'd rather not talk about it."

"So, what are you going to do?"

I raise an eyebrow. "About?"

His eyes widen. "Cami. Duh."

I shrug. Mostly, I've just been cursing the space she's taken up in my head. "I wasn't planning to do anything." She's a forever kind of woman, and I don't want to let her down by trying something with her and then falling short.

He rolls his eyes. "For a smart guy, you're an idiot about women. Luckily for you, I happen to know that she'll be at Mercy's tattoo parlor at 2:00 p.m. on Friday. Bet she could use some company."

My stomach flips. "Tattoo parlor?"

"Yeah." He grins. "She's getting her first ink."

My lips part as dozens of images flash through my mind. Camile's soft, satiny skin beneath a needle. Sexy ink decorating her already breathtaking body. Where would she get it? Back? Legs? Arms? Somewhere else…?

I take a deep breath and nod to Tony. "Thanks."

Perhaps I hadn't planned a next step, but I can't let her face something like her first tattoo alone. Come Friday, I'll be at that tattoo parlor. No matter how bad I might be for her, it seems I can't stay away.

4

I stand outside the tattoo place, staring up at the name above the door. Mercy Tattoos. I never thought to ask what it meant, but now that I'm here, with nerves crowding my stomach, I can't help but wonder. I smooth my sweaty palms down my top and gather my courage. I *want* this. I've thought long and hard about it. Karson's voice whispers in the back of my mind that tattoos on women are trashy, and I set my jaw. Fuck him. I'm doing this. I push the door open and step inside.

"Hi." I smile at the woman behind the counter. "I'm here for a 2:00 p.m. appointment. Camile Hayes."

She checks her screen and nods. "Sure thing, sweetie. Why don't you take a seat over there?" She points at a pair of sofas in the corner I didn't notice when I came in. "Mercy will be with you soon."

So Mercy is a person? Thank God.

A hulking figure sprawled on one of the sofas distracts me. *Leo.*

"What are you doing here?" I sit on the other sofa, keeping as much space between us as possible.

"I'm here for you." He straightens, and for once, I can't see the usual disdain in his expression. In fact, he looks almost nervous. "I heard from Tony that you're getting a tattoo, and I thought you might need some support." His Adam's apple bobs. "I figured Karson wouldn't be here for you."

Pleasure fizzes in my belly, and I try to tamp it down, but my stupid crush won't be ignored. It rears its head, desperate for any sign of his affection, real or imagined.

"Karson has no idea I'm here," I confess. "I've hardly spoken to him since… well, you know."

His brows knit together. "I thought you guys were connected at the hip."

I scoff, even though most people believe that exact thing. "I'm angry at him for what he did. It's not okay."

His eyes widen and he leans closer. "The drugs?"

"Yeah. But not just that. He always talked down about people who needed an extra edge to compete in the big leagues, and now it turns out he's a cheat." I let the air whistle through my teeth. "What a hypocrite."

Leo just looks at me for a moment, and I can see the cogs turning in his head, but then he nods in acknowledgment and changes the subject. "So, do you have anyone coming to keep you company?"

"No." I fiddle with the hem of my shirt. Being around him makes me nervous. Especially when he's so cordial. I'm used to his scornful glances—or being overlooked completely. This sudden interest is throwing me off. "Why are you here?"

He cocks his head. "I told you. I thought you might want company."

"You've never shown any interest in keeping me

company before. In fact, you seemed pretty eager to get rid of me the other day."

His shoulders sink. "You're right. I was a dick, and I'm sorry about that. I've been judging you based on Karson, and I'm beginning to think that was a mistake."

The admission surprises me. I know Leo likes to see things in black and white, so for him to admit he might have missed some shades of gray matters. "Perhaps," I agree. "But you might not have been totally wrong either." Interest flares in his eyes, and heat shoots to my core in response. I tell myself it doesn't mean anything, but my subconscious isn't listening. "You don't need to stay. I can handle this alone."

He smiles, and it might be the first honest smile he's ever given me. Golden and glorious. God, he's devastatingly handsome. "I want to be here. If that's okay with you."

I glance down at my hands because I can't handle the intensity of his gaze. Do I want him here? He stirs up such mixed emotions in me. But I'm admittedly nervous and having moral support, in whatever form it comes, surely can't hurt. "Thank you. It would be nice to have someone to take my mind off the whole needle thing."

"Hello."

We both turn at the sound of a voice, and my jaw drops. I whimper a little bit. Standing in front of me is one of the hottest specimens of manhood I've ever seen. His artfully tousled black hair falls around his face, shaping a chiseled jaw. He holds out a hand toward me, and the muscles of his colorfully-tattooed forearm flex. The eyes that settle on me are a startling shade of blue— so pale it's almost unnatural.

"You must be Camile." He continues holding his hand out and smiles. Goose bumps break out over my flesh. "I'm Mercy. I'll be doing your tattoo today."

It might be my imagination, but I think I hear Leo growl. Jolting back to reality, I shake Mercy's hand. The moment he releases me, I touch the corner of my mouth to make sure I'm not drooling.

"Hey." Mercy turns to Leo. "Leo Delaney, right?"

Leo nods and reluctantly offers a hand, which Mercy takes. "I'm here to sit with Cami. Unless that's a problem?"

I hide a smile at how petulant he sounds. Is he honestly bothered by another good-looking man? Mercy might be attractive, but he can't hold a candle to Leo.

"Not at all." Mercy jerks his head toward the tattoo booth. "Why don't both of you come on back?"

The receptionist winks at me as we pass, and I smile shyly.

"I've had a look at the scanned version of the design you sent me," Mercy says, and gestures for me to sit on what looks like a massage table. "Did you bring a physical copy?"

I perch on the edge and watch Leo drag a chair over to join us. "Yes." I fish the sketchpad from my purse and flip it open to the correct page before handing it over. My heart is in my throat as I watch him study it. I don't show my designs to people often, and my old insecurities are flaring up.

He makes a humming sound and finally looks at me. "It's even more beautiful in person. Did you draw this?"

"Yes," I whisper.

He grins. "You could have a future in tattooing, Cami."

I don't miss the way he uses my nickname, and based on how Leo stiffens, neither does he. I fight the urge to roll my eyes as I realize Leo keeps acting like he's not interested in me until he thinks another man might be. My jaw clenches and I try to ignore the tingles between my legs. Hot as it is to think he's getting possessive over me, he has no right to, and the last thing I need is another man who wants to run my life because he thinks he knows best.

"Are you happy for me to draw this onto you free-hand, or would you rather I trace it onto transfer paper to make sure we get it how you want?"

"You can go straight onto my skin," I tell him. Everyone says Mercy Tattoos is the best in the business, and if Mercy is its namesake, then I'm sure he's amazing. Besides, what's the point in stepping outside my comfort zone if I don't take a few risks along the way?

"Great." He dons gloves and rubs an antiseptic wipe over my forearm. "Would you prefer to lie down or sit up?"

"I'll lie down, just in case." I stretch out on the table, and he rearranges me into a position that works for him. I hear the hum of the needle, but I can't bear to look so I meet Leo's eyes instead. They're softer than I expect. Almost tender.

"You're doing well," he murmurs. "I didn't know you draw. How did you get into it?" He's trying to distract me, and I'm grateful. I'm so preoccupied that I don't flinch when the needle bites into my skin. My body stiffens for a moment, but then I relax into it. The pain isn't so bad. Uncomfortable, but not awful. I giggle to myself. Maybe I'm tougher than I thought.

Leo

She laughs. The crazy woman actually laughs when the tattoo artist buzzes the gun over her skin. I shake my head in disbelief. Camile Hayes is far from the person I thought she was. At first, I was annoyed she wouldn't stay in the box I put her in, but now I'm beginning to enjoy her unpredictability. I can't wait to see what she'll do or say next. It's as though she's had everything under lock and key for years, and suddenly she's thrown open the doors and decided to let her real self out.

"Cami," I prompt when she doesn't answer my question. "Where did you learn to draw?"

"Oh." She blushes and steals a glance at the tattoo gun, then goes pale and looks away. "I taught myself. I always loved drawing when I was younger. I suppose I probably picked up a few things through school, but mostly I just figured out what I liked and what I didn't."

"Wow." Her skills are impressive for someone who hasn't studied art.

"I have a diploma in fashion design," she adds cautiously, as though expecting me to look down my nose at her. Me? I punch people for a living. It's not as though I have any right to be snobby about anyone else's career aspirations. "I like designing clothes. It's fun. These days, I don't draw much outside of that."

"Nice." Mercy breaks into our conversation, and I want to tell him to shut up because I saw the way she looked at him before, and the idea of her fluttering those big blue eyes at anyone other than me makes me want to kick something. Like the hapless tattooist. But I'm not a violent person outside of the cage, and I know I'm being ridiculous, especially given I've been lecturing myself about the fact she's off-limits, so I rein in the impulse. "What kind of stuff do you design?"

She bites her lower lip. "Mostly dresses, tops, and skirts for plus-size women. I'm working on a plan to get them out into the world."

"That's great." He grins at her. "You ever have any

luck, let me know, okay? My sister is always complaining that she can't find any dresses that fit her chest without making her ass look massive." He pulls a face. "I wouldn't know, but I'm sure she'd be keen to have a look at anything you come up with."

"Thanks, I will." Her smile is shy. "But it might not be her style."

"Still worth a shot," I tell her. "I'm sure she'd love it. Have I seen anything you've designed?"

The pink of her cheeks deepens. "I design most of my own outfits."

"You do?" My gaze journeys down her body, noting the way the pale blue blouse lovingly cups her tits and then nips in before a darker skirt flares over her hips. It's a good look on her. Then again, her curves drive me insane regardless of what she's wearing. "That's awesome."

"Thank you." She starts to lower her chin, but then seems to catch herself and raises it back up. "My goal is to help women and girls realize they don't have to be thin to be beautiful."

"Amen to that," Mercy says. "How's the pain? Not too bad?"

She shakes her head. "It's okay."

After that, the conversation diverts to the latest fights. It turns out Mercy is an MMA-buff, which makes me feel slightly warmer toward him. But it seems Camile knows her stuff too. All that time she spent in the audience at fight events, I never realized how much she took in. She's like a sponge that's been soaked full of knowledge, and I can tell it impresses Mercy just as much as me. So does the fact she sits still while he etches a complicated lace bracelet pattern into her skin. She doesn't utter a single complaint. I suck in a deep breath and release it slowly. Camile Hayes is much more complex than I thought.

When her tattoo is finished and Mercy has given her instructions for after care, I'm not ready to say goodbye to her yet. I know I should. I don't want to lead her on and make her think I have more to offer than I actually do. But for some reason, I want to take care of her. She's grown steadily paler over the past hour, and I suspect she's worn out and needs sugar and something warm.

We leave the parlor and she turns to face me. "It was thoughtful of you to come."

I shrug because I can't exactly tell her I hadn't been able to stomach the thought of not seeing her again. "No big deal."

"Well, I'd better"

"Would you like to get coffee?" I ask at the same time as she speaks.

One of her brows lifts. "Now?"

"Yeah." I jam my hands into my pockets before I do something stupid like grab her and refuse to let go. "You should have a hot drink and something sweet. It'll be good for you after the shock your body's had."

She dithers for a moment, and I think she's going to refuse, but then she nods. "Okay. Why not?"

"Great." Relief soaks into my veins. I can't put my finger on why Camile has suddenly become so impor-tant to me, but there's no denying she has. "I'll drive, then I'll drop you off at home. You took an Uber here, right?"

She confirms, but gives me a look as though she's trying to figure out what my deal is. I can't say I blame her. I lead her to my car, and we drive to my favorite cafe in relative silence. There's so much I want to ask her, but I hold off until we're seated opposite each other at a small table, awaiting our drinks.

"Don't take this the wrong way," she begins, "but why do you keep appearing in my life? We've hardly had anything to do with each other for years, and now, all of a sudden, you're there every time I turn around."

I laugh because honestly, it feels like that for me too, only in reverse. "No offense taken." I rest my chin on my palm and lean toward her. "I'm intrigued. First the kiss, then the tattoo. Now I find out you're a clothing designer. Have you always done that kind of thing and I've just been oblivious, or has something changed?"

She ducks her head. "I've always been like that on the inside."

"But?" I prompt.

She squirms in her seat. I wait quietly but don't push her. "I guess..." She takes a deep breath and exhales slowly, then begins again. "When Karson got arrested, it shook me. It was awful, but it also made me realize how dependent I'd become on him and how I'd been putting off things that really mattered to me. So I made a list of activities I've always wanted to do and decided to go for it. Life is too short not to, you know?"

My heart beats a rapid rhythm. I have to admit, I want to know more. "What's on your list?"

5

For a moment, I wish the ground would open up and swallow me whole. I don't want to admit what's on my list to this gorgeous, confident man. But then, I'm practicing being brave and owning who I am, and this is the perfect opportunity to do just that. I bring the list up on my phone and hand it to him. He makes a sound in the back of his throat while he reads it.

"Why do you need to make a friend?"

Despite my cheeks heating to two million degrees, I manage not to bury my face in my hands. "Because I'd like to have one, and I don't at the moment."

He frowns. "That can't be right. What about Tony, or the people from CFC? Or surely you have a friend at work?"

"No." The admission deflates me because it's embarrassing as hell. What kind of woman in her late twenties doesn't have at least one close friend? "I have people I get on well with, but no one I'd call if I was upset at three o'clock in the morning."

"That's your threshold for friendship?" he asks.

A server chooses that moment to appear with a black coffee for Leo and a latte for me. I pause while she places them on the table, then when she's gone, I pour two packets of sugar into mine and stir.

"I don't want a friend for the sake of having a friend," I tell him. "I want someone to ride all the ups and downs with me. Someone who can be my rock, and I'll be theirs."

His lips quirk. "Sounds like you're looking for a relationship more than a friendship."

I lift one shoulder and let it fall. "I'll take a friend in whatever form they come."

I can tell he wants to say something, but to my surprise, he holds back. Instead, he taps a finger against the phone screen. "You can cross off one and two."

I roll my eyes, amused he assumes his kiss counts as my mind-blowing kiss. It does, but I'd never admit it to his face.

He passes the phone back and cradles his coffee between both palms. "I'll go ziplining with you."

"I didn't think you liked me." I slap a hand to my mouth, but the words are already out. I groan in mortification. "I mean…." I straighten my shoulders. No pussy-footing around. "No, that's exactly what I mean. I understand what you said earlier about judging me based on Karson, but it's kind of hard to ignore the fact that apart from today, you haven't given the impression you think much of me as a person."

He looks put on the spot, but I don't let up. I've spent years believing he thinks poorly of me for no good reason, so he deserves to suffer a moment of discomfort. His expression softens, and he lays a hand on mine. "To be honest, I don't think I've ever had any idea who you really are." He squeezes gently. "And you can't dislike what you don't know. I just didn't approve of the way you seemed to fit yourself around Karson's life. It was as though you couldn't think for yourself. You deferred to him for everything."

I hang my head because he isn't wrong. I *did* do that. I put Karson on a pedestal he didn't deserve. "Yeah. I can see how you'd think of me as an airhead follower type."

"Cami, look at me."

I raise my eyes.

"I'm glad you're finally doing something for yourself. Whatever happens with Karson, don't stop being you, okay?"

"I won't," I promise, and know deep down it's the truth. I can't go back. Everything has changed, and rewinding the clock would be impossible.

"So." He straightens and removes his hand from mine. I feel a pang in my heart at the loss. "You said you're working on a plan for your clothing design. Will you tell me about it?"

He's clearly hoping to lighten the mood, and while I suppose it's working to a certain extent, design is something that's very close to my heart. "I've been planning to pitch my designs to a clothing company for months now, but there are a couple of things that keep holding me back." I sip my latte, enjoying the rush of sweetness because I'm still a little shaky from getting the tattoo. Distracted by that thought, I glance down at my forearm and smile at the design wrapping around it. "It came out really well, didn't it?"

"Yeah," he agrees. "What's been holding you back?"

"Oh." I look away from my arm. "Just that I've been scared they won't be good enough, or that if I sell them to a company, they'd want to change them without consulting me." I smile wryly. "Perhaps it's egotistical, but I like my designs the way they are, and I don't want anyone messing with them."

"I get that. I can imagine many artists feel the same way when someone buys the rights to commercialize their work."

An artist. Is that how he sees me? I love the thought. I consider myself creative, but I've never been brave enough to claim the title "artist."

"It's not just that," I explain. "I spend a lot of time figuring out what will make plus-size women feel good about themselves, and a few changes in the wrong direction could totally undermine that."

He stares at me, and maybe it's my imagination, but his blue eyes seem to get hotter and darker. A slow heat builds low in my belly. I shift in my chair and squeeze my thighs together, trying to ease the ache. "I think you'd be selling yourself short if you gave your designs to someone else." His voice is husky and sends a shiver through my body. "You'd be better off pitching to an investor who's willing to finance you to launch your own line, on your own terms."

I laugh, because honestly, what kind of investor would be willing to give me money? I have no track record, no practical experience, and no reputation. I'm a nobody. If anyone cared to Google my name, all they'd see is I'm the twin sister of an athlete whose reputation is currently being dragged through the mud.

But I still can't help but wonder what it would be like to run a show myself. I allow myself a moment to fantasize. I've dreamed about it for years and I have so many ideas. But surely even considering the option is crazy, right?

"Seriously," I urge. "At least try it. The worst they can do is say no."

Camile's face scrunches and she looks like she wants to point out a dozen ways I'm wrong. "They would probably laugh at me," she mutters. "It's not like I'm much of an entrepreneur."

"How do you know that?"

She blinks slowly. "I barely passed math."

"So?" I challenge, mentally sifting through ideas to fire her up. "Do you think that Chanel lady pours over the accounts each day? I bet she hires someone to do it for her because her time is too precious. Being an entrepreneur doesn't mean you have to do everything yourself. It means finding the right people to fill the gaps." I can see she's listening to me, so I barrel on. "What are you really afraid of?"

She catches her lower lip between her teeth, and my dick starts to thicken in response, but I will it to calm the fuck down. Now isn't the time to get carried away. I'd just freak her out. I'm already pushing the boundaries, having shown up at the tattoo parlor without an invitation and then talking her into coming for coffee. At this point, I have no idea what I'm doing, but I don't want this to be the last time I see her.

"What if I suck?" she asks. "If a clothing company turns me down, I can tell myself it's because my designs aren't a good fit. But if an investor does the same, it's because they don't think I'm a good investment. Those people know a lot about business. I don't know if I could handle it if I put my best foot forward and they weren't interested."

My heart aches for her because clearly nobody has ever given her their unwavering faith, but at the same time, her attitude frustrates me. She's full of talk about being her own person and going after what she wants, but she's letting her old fears and insecurities hold her back. If she takes a punt without having her whole soul in it, I worry it will turn out as she's predicted because it'll be obvious to anyone listening that she doesn't believe in herself. If that's the case, why would they be willing to take a chance on her? But something tells me I need to be gentle, or she'll retreat into her shell.

"What if you don't suck?" I ask quietly. "What if they love you and give you everything you need to make your dream come true? Isn't it worth risking a few minutes of pain?"

She cocks her head. "What if it's a few days of pain? Or weeks? Because let's be real, I'm not the sort of person who bounces back quickly."

"Then you have a few days or weeks of pain." I shrug. "Worst-case scenario, you'll still survive." I straighten, deciding it's time to end the conversation while I'm ahead. I've stirred her thoughts. Hopefully she can muster enough confidence in herself to do something about it. "It's your choice. Do whatever you think is best. Just make sure you're doing it because it's what you want."

"I will." She nibbles her lip again, and this time, I can't resist the urge to reach over and smooth a thumb across it. She freezes. So do I. What was I thinking? I can't touch her like that. She's not for me. But to my surprise, she doesn't flinch. I retract my thumb, which is still tingling from her lips. "Would you like to see what I've been working on?"

My stomach lurches, and my heart takes off. "I thought you hadn't showed anyone before?"

"I haven't." She smiles tentatively. "But I'd like you to be the first."

"Absolutely." I may not have had any interest in

women's fashion before today, but when it comes to Camile, I want to know everything. "I'd love that."

"Great. Can you drive me back to my place?"

She doesn't mean that the way it sounds. But damn, my body wishes she did.

"No problem."

We finish our drinks and head to the car. She directs me to an apartment building, and we park in the basement. As we climb the stairs, I sense her body tensing with each step.

"Are you sure you want to do this?" I ask as we leave the stairwell and enter a corridor.

"Absolutely." Her tone is firm with no sign of the quiver I see in her hands. "It's this one." She stops outside a door. "Excuse the mess. I don't have visitors often, and I can get a little carried away when I'm on a roll."

I hide a smile. I doubt Camile's mess is anything compared to some of the guys I've lived with. But my eyes widen as the door swings open. Holy crap. It's not so much that the place is a mess. It's more that pieces of paper and scraps of fabric cover nearly every surface. I don't even know where to start looking. There must be dozens of designs littering the table and floor. I cross to the coffee table, figuring that's where she's most likely to keep whatever she's currently working on. As gently as possible, I touch one of the sheets of paper and orient it so I can see what I'm looking at. A flowing dress with a low-cut front is sketched in the same careful lines as the tattoo design had been. Even with my limited experience, I can tell the outfit would look beautiful on her.

"This is amazing," I breathe, and scan another piece of paper. Then another. With each new design, my admiration increases. Eventually, I stop and face her. "You're really fucking talented."

She blushes and bites her lower lip. "You think?"

I nod. "These should be on display. There's no doubt in my mind that someone would pay you to make these."

Her smile nearly blinds me with its brilliance. "Thank you." The air leaves her in a gust. "I always thought they were nice, but it's kind of hard to judge your own work."

"Don't ever doubt yourself again." Before I can think about it, I grab her and kiss those pouty lips of hers. They taste just as good as they did on Sunday, and when she gives a little gasp of surrender, my cock stiffens to the point of discomfort. I rock forward, then freeze and force myself to back off. God, I can't go humping her like an animal. We might be getting on well, but she's shy and skittish—at least, she is when she's not handing me my ass. "You're good." I brush one more kiss over her mouth so she knows I don't think it was a mistake. I may not know what I'm doing kissing her when I should be leaving her alone, but no matter how wise my actions, she could never be a mistake. "Really good."

"You have no idea what a relief it is to hear you say that." She smiles slyly. "Even if you're not exactly an expert on fashion."

I narrow my eyes at the saucy comment, but my heart lifts. I love when she teases me. "I could be an expert if I wanted to be."

She rolls her eyes. "Sure you could." She saunters across the room, her hips swaying, and settles onto the sofa. "So, what say we make a plan for ziplining?"

6

Leo

Camile and I message each other constantly over the course of the next week. I keep telling myself to play it cool and slow down—reminding myself I haven't had the best role models for relationships and I should stop before I hurt her—but every morning, without fail, I think of her and I'm unable to concentrate until I get in touch. She's sweet, and sometimes funny. But it's her moments of sass I love the most. When they come out, it takes every bit of my control not to tell her all the dirty things I want to do to her. Not that I really know how to flirt or talk dirty. It's been so long since I tried. But that's okay, because she seems a bit rusty too, and we're figuring this out together.

Smack!

Enya's fist hits me in the face, and I automatically raise my arms to block any further punches. We're at Crown MMA Gym, sparring, and I've let myself drift into another world yet again.

"Get your head in the game," she snaps. "You're distracted."

She's annoyed. In her shoes, I would be too. She needs to train, and I'm putting in a shitty performance. She deserves better. Enya has never won a major championship. She gets within a hairbreadth of the win, only to have it snatched away every time. Now, in our new gym, she has renewed energy. Seth Isles has got her doing weights every second day and it shows. She packs a lot more power than she used to. But no matter how much heart she has—and it's a fuck ton more than most men—she's going to be crushed if she doesn't get the win that's been eluding her. Seth has mentioned a promising lead for her and she wants it badly.

"Sorry, En."

Her nostrils flare and she thwacks a kick toward my rib cage, looking mollified when I check it and strike back with a push kick. For the remainder of the round, I force myself to give my training buddy the attention she needs. When the beeper sounds, we bump gloves.

She shakes her head. "You've been daydreaming all week. What's going on?"

My cheeks heat. "Nothing."

She squints. "Are you blushing?" Her mouth drops open. "Is this about a girl?"

"Shh," I hiss. The last thing I need is a bunch of well-meaning assholes teasing me about my crush. "I've been talking to Camile."

I wait for her to make some snarky comment about Camile's relation to Karson, but she doesn't. Her delicate eyebrows pull toward the bridge of her nose. "I thought you didn't like Camile."

I rub a palm down my face. I hate the fact that everyone seems to know I didn't think much of Camile before now. "I was an ass. I made assumptions before I got to know her. I'm fixing that."

To my surprise, she grins. "Cami, huh? I always wondered what your type was."

"I don't have a type," I say too quickly. I totally do. Curvy blondes with kissable lips and eyes like the sky on a clear summer day.

"Uh-huh." She winks. "Your secret is safe with me." She mimes zipping her lips. "Do you have any plans with her?"

I shuffle on the spot, wondering how much to admit. "We're going ziplining on Saturday." I've been looking forward to it ever since I kissed her goodbye. In hindsight, I should have made plans with her earlier in the week because I've been dying to see her. Unfortunately, I don't know for sure whether she feels the same way. She seemed to enjoy kissing me, but she holds her cards close to her chest. To be fair, so do I.

"Ziplining?" Enya's face lights up. "Is it an official date?"

"No." I should have known she'd be interested. While she may not appear it because of her girl-next-door looks, Enya is an adrenaline junkie. "I'm taking it slow. I don't want to come on too strong." I wince, wondering how much to say. "I haven't had many relationships, and I'm worried I might hurt her."

Her expression softens. "Like your dad does to your mom?"

"Exactly."

She bops me on the shoulder. "I get why you're concerned, but you don't need to be. From what I understand, your dad was a party boy to the core. You're different from him in so many ways. You'd never do that to anyone."

Her words warm me. Could it be that she's right? I did earn my nickname because I don't sleep around, and it's not as if I've been tempted by other women since I've been talking to Camile. My heart lifts. Maybe I can make this work. It's worth trying.

"Thanks, En. You're the best."

"I know." She flashes her hundred-megawatt smile. "Back to the ziplining. Would it be all right if I come, or would I be intruding? We could make it a group thing. Take the pressure off."

"That should be okay." Honestly, I'd rather have Camile to myself. But maybe she'll feel more comfortable if there's a group of us rather than just her and me. "I'll check and let you know."

"Thanks. I should have known that good old Priest would be the first of us to succumb to the Crown MMA love disease."

I huff. "Not true."

Enya is convinced there's something in the water here that makes people go gaga in love. So far, the five of us who moved from City Fight Center have been unaffected, but I can see she's going to grab on to this and use it to fuel her suspicions.

"Yes, true," she teases. "I can't wait to see you fall."

⁂

CAMILE

I wish I had a friend I could have girl talk with. Leo and I have been keeping in touch all week, and I practically leap with excitement every time the phone buzzes in case it's him. The only problem is, I'm not sure whether my feelings are reciprocated. I mean, logically, it seems like he wouldn't waste his time messaging me so much if he weren't interested, but I don't really know what to expect from men. My limited sexual experiences have been more of the one-night stand variety. The first time, I thought I was in the early stages of a whirlwind love affair, but when the afterglow cooled and he asked me to introduce him to Karson, I received a cold dose of reality. I stayed away from men I met at fight events after that. The second time I'd had sex, it was after I'd been stood up by an online date. I'd ended up chatting with a man who was crying at the bar. His girlfriend had broken up with him. He'd wanted comfort, and I'd wanted to be wanted. So we went back to his place. Then, filled with shame, I'd snuck out in the middle of the night.

I choose my outfit carefully. I want to look nice, but I can't wear a dress or skirt or I'll flash someone, so I opt for a pair of dark jeans and a blouse. Strangely enough, I'm more nervous about being around a group of people from the gym than I am about hurtling through the air. When Leo asked if I minded a few others joining us, I was disappointed. I'd looked forward to being alone with him. But I'd agreed anyway. Maybe I'll find that friend I desperately want. Although, considering how much I don't have in common with anyone who fights for a living, I doubt it.

As I drive to the meeting point, I mull over what Leo's friends—Karson's former crew—probably think of me. I can't imagine it's anything good. They've only ever met me through my brother. Sigh.

I park and search for an elevator because I'd rather not be a sweaty mess when Leo sees me. According to the message he sent earlier, he's already here. My phone pings again as I step into the elevator, and I check the screen.

Mom: *Karson needs you. Please stop punishing him like this.*

I pocket the phone and ignore a pang of guilt. I'm not punishing him, am I? I'm just doing what I should have been all along. Right?

The elevator glides to a halt, and the doors slowly open. I step onto the rooftop, shielding my eyes from the sun. A group of people are gathered near a booth a hundred feet away and I wander over, trying not to notice how high we are. Nerves sing in my chest. Much as I want to do this, I'm also slightly scared of heights.

"Hey, Cami."

I blink rapidly as my vision adjusts, and I see Leo approaching. "Hi."

He kisses my cheek and my hormones go haywire. He smells so good. After texting him all week, I feel like I know him reasonably well, but a niggling insecurity tells me not to read too much into his affection.

Enya Sears bounds over and punches Leo lightly on the arm. "Don't keep her all to yourself, big guy." Her doe-like eyes sparkle with humor and intelligence. When Leo smiles and jostles her shoulder affectionately, my internal voice of doubt builds until it's practically yelling in my ears.

"As if anyone could ignore you, En," he teases.

I watch them interact. I've never known what to make of Enya. She's always welcoming, but we've never talked to each other much. I wouldn't even know where to begin making conversation with her. She's beloved by half the country and clearly has no trouble owning who she is. She's my opposite. Athletic where I'm curvy. Freckled and brunette while I'm a pale blonde. Sure of her place in a world where I've never quite felt I belong.

I swallow my disappointment. Is it possible that while I'm busy crushing on Leo, he's more interested in Enya? They'd certainly make more sense as a couple, but the thought makes me want to cry, so I brush it away.

"Hi." I smile tightly. I wish I could muster something

more genuine, but thanks to my envy, I just can't. "It's nice to see you."

"You too." Her answering smile has all the warmth mine lacks. "Thanks for letting us tag along. I haven't done this zipline before, although I've ridden a couple of others."

Leo chuckles. "Enya is addicted to adrenaline. If you can jump off it or out of it, she's there."

Of course. So while I'm here to make a statement about reclaiming my life, she goes around doing this kind of thing regularly. I hope Leo hasn't mentioned my list to her, or I'll never be able to look her in the eye again. I have a long way to go before we're on the same playing field. But then the tightness in my chest eases because Leo's eyes crinkle in a smile meant just for me. I'm being ridiculous. He wouldn't have mentioned my list, and I have no reason to be jealous. They've trained together for years. If they wanted to date, they would have.

Get a grip, Cami. Don't be one of those brats who can't stand to be around successful women.

"He's exaggerating." To my surprise, Enya shoos Leo away with one hand. "Go. Let me talk to Cami for a minute."

He glances between us, hesitating, but then nods. "I'll join Tony and Jimmy." He grabs my hand and squeezes before walking over to join his friends. I watch his back as he goes and sigh.

"Oh my God," Enya whispers. "You're just as goofy as he is!"

My eyes snap to hers. "Excuse me?"

She winks. "He's been driving me crazy all week. Every time his phone makes a noise, he wants to check it immediately, and then he gets this ridiculous grin." She mimics him, and I stifle a laugh. "Honestly, I want to give him a hard time about it because he's acting like a lovesick fool, but he never does anything like this, and I'd hate to make him self-conscious." She pats me on the shoulder. "I'm happy for you both. He needs something good in his life to take his mind off the trouble we've been dealing with since the bust, and I'm sure you do too." Her grip tightens. "But if you break his heart, we're going to have problems. Got it?"

I stare at her mutely, and she starts to turn away but then I stop her. "You think I could break his heart?"

She rolls her eyes. "The guy can't take his eyes off you." She glances at him, and I follow her gaze. Sure enough, he's looking straight at us. "He's in deep."

"I am too," I admit. "I just wasn't sure whether I'm the only one."

Her expression softens. "You're not."

"Thanks, Enya." This conversation hasn't gone anything like I expected, and now I can't help but wonder how Enya would feel about being *my* friend as well as Leo's.

"Hey, bellissima." Tony makes a show of kissing each of my cheeks as we join the men. I sense them heat and know I must be red-faced, but he doesn't seem to care. Instead, he steals a peek at Leo and laughs. "Easy, Priest. I'm not trying to steal your girl."

Flutters erupt in my belly. *His girl?* Is that what I am? I'd certainly like to be, but all we've shared are a few kisses. I wait for Leo to protest. He doesn't. In fact, the desire in his gaze turns my insides to jelly. Finally, I'm certain. We're both in this, and I don't know where it's going, but I'm happy to be along for the ride.

"Is this all of you?" the zipline operator asks.

"Yes." The only man I don't know is the one to answer. I assume he's Jimmy. The guy is in his early twenties, with long, golden hair twisted into a bun at the back of his head and scruff on his jaw.

When the operator starts grabbing gear, Enya claps her hands in delight. Based on the way Jimmy watches her hungrily, he wants to be more than her teammate, but she seems completely oblivious. The operator introduces himself, but my nerves are going crazy so I don't hear what he says.

"Who's going first?" he asks. "We've got two ziplines that run in parallel, so you can go two at a time."

Leo looks at me, but I shake my head. I need another couple of minutes to work on my confidence. Enya steps forward and almost immediately, Jimmy does the same. My lips quirk. His less-than-subtle crush is pretty cute. The operator connects them to the lines and issues instructions. I hold my breath as the pair soar from the rooftop and over the city streets.

"Our turn," Leo says, taking my hand.

My head spins dizzyingly. "But what about Tony?"

Tony waves a hand. "I don't mind going by myself."

"Okay." I clench my jaw and step up. A tremble runs through my body as the operator secures a harness around me, and I can't tell if it's from nerves or excitement.

"First time?" he asks.

"Yeah." The word comes out shaky. "Is it that obvious?"

"Kinda." He winks. "But don't worry, it'll be fun. It's like flying."

"That's what I'm hoping for."

He tests the harness and then releases it and does the same for Leo. I do my best to listen while he explains what will happen next, but my pulse is drumming loud enough I can barely hear him. I step right up to the edge at the same time as Leo and make the mistake of looking down. The world swims before my eyes as tiny, ant-like figures scurry back and forth on the pavement below. Someone touches my hand and I flinch. When I look up, I find Leo watching me.

"You got this." He leans over and kisses me, hard and fast. "Let's go."

And then, while I'm still dazed from his kiss, I step off the edge of the building. The terror lasts for only a few seconds before exhilaration takes over. My eyes leak as the wind stings them, but I absolutely love it. I spread my arms and whoop as buildings pass by in a blur.

Now *this* is living.

7

I barely notice the buildings fly by. My attention is centered on the beautiful woman zipping along beside me. Even though her eyes are streaming, they're bright with joy. I can't believe I never looked past my assumptions to see who she is on the inside. I've been missing out on Camile, and if I'd only been a little less black-and-white in my judgment, and a little more willing to take a chance, we might have been getting to know each other for years now. But I didn't, and I have to live with that. The best I can do is move forward the way I wish I had in the past and try really hard not to screw up.

We slow as we reach the end, hovering a couple of feet above the ground. An operator unclips Camile and then me. I get to my feet and grab the harness for balance when my legs wobble beneath me. I turn to check on Camile and find her beaming. My breath catches in my throat. Fuck, she's stunning.

"How'd you like that?" I ask.

She jumps up and down a couple of times and

squeals. "Best. Thing. Ever. I'm totally coming back next weekend."

"It's addictive, right?" the operator says.

"Is it ever." She throws her arms around me. "Thanks for coming. It's so much better to have company."

"No problem." I bury my face in her hair and inhale her scent. "Mm."

She stiffens. "Did you just sniff me?"

"No," I lie.

She laughs. "Oh my God. You did."

I pull back and smile at her sheepishly. "You smell amazing."

She blushes. "Uh, thanks. But we should probably get out of the way."

"Oh yeah." I'd forgotten Tony would be arriving at any moment. We move to the side but don't join Enya and Jimmy yet. I can't take my eyes off Camile's mouth. I want to kiss her again so badly.

"You're staring at me," she whispers.

"You're nice to look at," I reply.

She just shakes her head as though I amuse her and takes my hand. "Come on." She leads me to the others.

"What did you think?" Enya asks as soon as we're close enough to speak without raising our voices.

"That was so much fun," Camile says. "I kinda want to look up the other ziplines in Vegas and do them all."

Enya grins. "If you're serious, I'd be keen to join you. I'm always up for something like that."

"Really?"

"Absolutely." Enya meets my eyes and winks. I love that she's making an effort to include Camile. I mouth "Thank you," and she gives me a look that says her friendliness has nothing to do with my dumb ass.

Jimmy holds up his hand for a high five, and Camile

slaps it after only a moment's hesitation. "Ready to go again?" he asks.

"Hell yeah."

I laugh at her enthusiasm. I could get used to this. We wait a few minutes until Tony whooshes into view. He slides to a stop and gets unhooked by the operator, then we crowd into the company's van. I slide into a window seat and draw Camile onto the spot beside me. To my surprise, she rests her cheek against my shoulder and settles in. My chest clenches. Yeah, I could definitely get used to this.

"Want to get a drink together?" Jimmy asks from somewhere behind me. "All of us, I mean?"

Camile snickers, although I'm not sure why.

"Would you like that?" I can see my training buddies any day. I'd rather spend time with her, whether that's at a bar or somewhere else.

"Sure."

"Count me in," Tony adds. "Although it'll have to be non-alcoholic since I'm in fight camp."

"Already?" Jimmy sounds surprised.

"No rest for the wicked." Tony turns from the seat in front of us and winks at Camile. "I'm *very* wicked."

"I just bet you are," she murmurs.

I glare at him. He gives me a cocksure grin. He's intentionally winding me up. Asshole. They unload us outside the building we took off from, but instead of going to find our cars, we walk down to the street to the nearest bar. The place is quiet since it's midafternoon. A couple of guys are playing pool in the corner, but other than that, it's empty. We order drinks—non-alcoholic for Tony and Enya—and gather around one of the bar leaners.

"What's that?" I ask Camile, tipping my head toward her shot glass of amber liquid.

The corners of her mouth curve mischievously. "Whiskey."

I laugh. "Of course it is." Probably something she's always wanted to order but never has. I raise my beer to her. "Bottoms up, princess."

She gulps the whiskey down a little too enthusiastically and sputters. "It burns!"

Tony, on the other side of her, cracks up. "It's whiskey. What'd you expect?"

She shakes her head but doesn't say anything. Meanwhile, Enya leans over to sniff the empty glass. "Mm. I miss whiskey."

Camile pulls a face. "You're welcome to it. In the future, I'm sticking with wine or cocktails." She stands. "In fact, I'm going to get something to wash that taste out of my mouth." She heads for the bar, and I watch her go, scowling when one of the guys playing pool checks out her ass.

"Somebody is smitten," Enya sings under her breath.

I don't bother to deny it. "She's pretty great."

When Camile returns a few minutes later with a radioactive pink drink, Jimmy smirks and opens his mouth to comment, but I shut him down with a glare. If that's what Camile wants, she should have it. Although, when she begins to loosen up and her touches become more frequent, I do have to wonder whether it was a good idea. She seems to find excuses to put her hands on me. Much as I love it, I'm having an awkward physical reaction and wish I could get her somewhere private. That doesn't seem likely with the conversation flowing so naturally.

At first, Camile is more of an observer than a participant, but once she begins to feel comfortable, she joins in. I wrap my arms around her from behind and touch my cheek to hers. Her ass presses into my groin and I bury my face in her shoulder to muffle a groan. The woman doesn't realize how sexy she is. If she doesn't stop moving, she's going to give me a publicly inappropriate boner. Tony chuckles as he notices my dilemma, but for once in his life, he doesn't take advantage of the opportunity to play the joker. Instead, he makes a show of looking at his phone.

"I've got to get home." He sends me a meaningful look.

"Me too." I give Camile a little squeeze, hoping she'll pick up on the message.

"Oh, uh, yeah. I have to go too." Her words are breathless. "I have a thing."

Enya cocks a brow. "A thing?"

"Uh-huh." Her cheeks are rapidly turning pink. "A, um, big thing that I need to do."

"A big thing, huh?" Tony smirks, and I'm torn between being embarrassed and thinking she's the most adorable person ever.

Reaching down, I thread my fingers through hers. "Let's get you home."

Enya looks at Jimmy and seems to realize they're about to be left on their own. "Okay. Time to go."

The group leaves together and walks to the zipline building's parking lot.

As we draw near to our destination, I brush my mouth over Camile's. "Can I come to your place?"

A shiver runs through her. "I'd like that."

***

Camile

When we enter my place, I'm pleased I cleaned up earlier. There are still designs everywhere, but I've stacked them in orderly piles so I can work through them and choose my favorites. I've decided to follow Leo's suggestion and pitch to investors first. While it has the potential to be hardest on my ego, I think there's a higher likelihood of success because venture capitalists don't mind taking a risk in a way that clothing companies may not. I've sorted through about half of the designs and have a growing pile of discards, but I'm really excited for the small array I've selected for my collection.

"Wow." Leo whistles as he enters behind me. "You've been busy."

I look over my shoulder and grin. "You inspired me."

I probably shouldn't be so frank, but the drinks at the bar have loosened my inhibitions enough to flirt with him and see where it leads. Based on the way he whispered hotly in my ear before we separated from the others, I have a good feeling about it. Leo takes my hand and guides me to the sofa separating the living area from the bed. I see him glance over at the rumpled blankets and then his gaze clashes with mine. The look in his eyes has butterflies erupting in my stomach. What will it feel like when he actually lays his hands on me?

He sits and pats the spot beside him. I sink into the sofa, my knees wobbling, and he curls his palm around the side of my face, sending ripples of desire through my body. The tip of his thumb presses into my lower lip, and he holds it there for a moment. Excitement pulses between my legs. He looks like the lion he's named for—hungry and ready to move in for the kill. I can't help but squirm while I wait for him to act.

Finally, he dips his head and his lips meet mine. Lightning flashes on the insides of my eyelids. The naughty pixies in my pants want to throw a party and invite him in. Nothing about the kiss is tentative. It's thorough, as though he's wringing as much pleasure as possible from every second. I sigh happily and press closer. He smells faintly of beer, but it's the scent of his skin that overwhelms me. It's pure Leo. Masculine, woodsy, and enticing.

I run my hand down his chest, over sculpted muscles, and down to the front of his jeans. He groans and thrusts his hips forward, hard behind his fly.

"Touch me," he murmurs. "Please."

I cup his erection, but before I can decide what to do next, he grabs my shoulders and jerks me toward him. I straddle his legs, then hesitate. While he's given no sign he doesn't like my size, I'm probably heavier than the other girls he's been with, and I'm worried I'll squish him. How unsexy would that be?

"You're thinking too hard." He reaches for the hem of my blouse. "Is this okay?"

"Wait."

He immediately drops the fabric. "What's going on in your head, Cami? Let me in."

"I, um." I bite my lip, afraid to share my fears even though I know realistically he's unlikely to say, "yeah, actually, you *are* too fat for me." I muster my courage. "I'm worried you won't be impressed with what you find beneath my clothes." I squeeze my eyes shut for a second but then force myself to open them again. "I have thick thighs and love handles. If you're not okay with that, then we can't go any further." When I'm finally brave enough to look him in the eyes, he's staring at me incredulously.

"You are the sexiest woman I've seen in my entire fucking life." His voice trembles with emotion. He raises a hand as if to brush hair from my face but stops short. "Have I done anything to make you think otherwise?"

I want to roll into a ball and hide, but I can't run away from this situation, and if I don't deal with it now, then the fear will only return with a vengeance later. "No, but I've had plenty of nasty things said to me, and it's kind of hard to forget them."

He frowns as understanding dawns. "Like the men at the club that night?"

"Yeah." I climb off and sit beside him. R.I.P. to the sexy mood.

But then Leo grasps my chin between his thumb and forefinger and turns my face toward him. "I wish I'd punched that asshole." His nostrils flare and his eyes burn with anger, but not directed at me. "I should have laid him the fuck out for speaking to you like that. I just…" He releases a shuddering breath. "I was trying to keep a low profile because of the whole drug thing. But it shouldn't have mattered." He studies me, trying to gauge my reaction. "I'm sorry I didn't do that for you."

I shrug as though every awful name those men called me didn't cut to my very bones. "You hardly knew me then."

He scoffs. "Doesn't matter. Nobody should be treated like they're trash." His lips brush mine and he nuzzles the side of my neck. I relax, and warmth fills me. He continues. "I've always thought you were gorgeous. But I'd mentally classified you as off-limits because of Karson."

I try not to flinch. Of course he did. Story of my life. I'm rarely judged on my own merits.

"We don't have to go any further if you don't want to," he says. "But I'd love to bury my face between those thick thighs you mentioned and make you forget about anyone who ever said anything mean to you."

My thighs clench tighter at his words, and my clit begs for his attention. "I want that."

He grins. "Then how about I strip off first so you feel less exposed and vulnerable?"

I nearly laugh. Yeah, seeing the man who's built like a Greek god naked isn't really going to make me feel less self-conscious. But I'm not about to pass up the opportunity to ogle him, so I keep my mouth shut while he stands and strips off his shirt and jeans, leaving him clad in only a pair of briefs that lovingly caress the bulge of his cock. My gaze journeys down his body, over the ridges of his abdomen and deep grooves above his hips. I swallow. There's a damp spot on his underwear, where precum has soaked through. Liquid heat rushes to my core. He really does like my body. So much that he's been leaking for me. My lips curl into a sultry smile. I feel like a seductress. Like the type of woman I never dreamed I could be.

"Look at you." He rubs a hand over his cock, and his pale eyes blaze into mine. "So damn hot. Will you take your clothes off for me?"

I reach out and trace the tip of a finger along the fabric between my skin and his hard length. "This first."

His chest rises and falls on a rough exhale. He peels down the underwear, revealing himself to me. His erection is thick and ruddy with a short thatch of blond hair at the base. As I watch, he wraps his palm around it and strokes. More precum drips from the head, and before I can think about it, I've dipped my hand between my legs to put pressure on my pussy.

"No," he grunts. "Don't touch yourself. That's my job. Now, will you please take off your clothes?"

Hearing his frustration, my confidence grows. I cross to him, but instead of doing what he's asked, I splay my hands on his abs and flick his tight brown nipple with my tongue. Breath hisses between his teeth. As I move to do the same to the other one, he snags a hand in my hair and yanks my head back, baring my throat. He drags his teeth over the skin there. It doesn't hurt, but he's clearly taking control of the encounter, and something about that sets me alight.

He travels to my jaw and then his mouth skims the surface of mine. "Stop playing with me, Cami. I need you."

I whimper and squeeze my thighs together. Leo is so hot, and in this moment, he's all mine. There's absolutely no doubt in my mind he means every word he says. I rub myself against him sensually. "Get on the bed."

He cocks his head. "You gonna make me?"

Startled, I back off a step, but then I take in the debauched image he presents and my confidence returns. His blond hair is mussed, his eyes glow with desire, and he's naked while I'm completely clothed.

Why? Why am I still wearing anything?

I fumble with my blouse, pulling it over my head, then undo my jeans and shimmy them down. Finally, I'm standing before him in nothing but a soft pink bra that does little to hide my breasts, and a matching set of panties.

"Fuck." He grabs my hand and urges me around the sofa and onto the bed. I lie down while he stands at the end. His gaze sweeps over me, setting my nerves ablaze. "You're so beautiful."

I run my hands over my breasts and to the clasp between, snapping it open. Right now, I *feel* beautiful, thanks to him. Leo kisses each of my breasts, murmuring quiet compliments that go straight to my heart. He slides down my body to make good on his earlier promise. His mouth settles over my pussy, and he licks the flesh softly at first, but then groans and laps harder. My hands fly to the back of his head to hold him in place and pleas spill from me.

Don't stop. More. Right there. Please.

He's merciless in the pursuit of my pleasure until the moment he has me teetering on the brink. But then, before I can come, he pulls back.

"No!" I protest.

He kisses my forehead. "Do you have a condom?"

"Uh." I pause to think. It's been a long time since I needed one. "Yes, top drawer of the dresser. But check the expiry date."

He opens the drawer and sifts through until he finds the box, then checks the back. "Good. Thank God." He tears the foil wrapper and rolls it over his length. "You with me, Cami?"

"Completely."

He climbs over me and nuzzles my neck. "You're gorgeous, baby."

He notches himself at my entrance and eases inside an inch at a time. I bite my lip as he fills me. It feels so good being this close to him. I hold his gaze and let him see how much I love what he's doing. I never imagined he'd be the one to make me feel so treasured, but I wouldn't have it any other way.

"Just like that," I urge.

He bottoms out and rests his forehead against mine, breathing heavily. "You're going to make me come in two minutes if I'm not careful."

Yes. The thought of breaking his strict control drives me crazy. My pussy clasps tighter around him. I rock my hips, riding him from below. He lets out a low moan.

"I've never wanted anyone as much as I want you," I confess.

"Neither." He thrusts in and out, and I throw my head back as his fingers delve between us and rub my clit. "You make me wild."

My mouth finds his, and there are no more words

between us. We exchange heated kisses, our breath intermingling, as sweat slicks our skin. My back arches as sensation zips up my spine, spiraling out of control. I know Leo can sense it because his jaw firms and moves harder and faster.

"Let go," he murmurs. "I've got you."

He pulses inside me, and it's all I need to plunge into the most magnificent orgasm of my life. A keening sound tears from my mouth, and I shudder beneath him. He drives into me over and over again, muttering my name every time. On one final thrust, he cries out his release. Ecstasy lines his face, and I can't take my eyes off him. After a moment, he settles on top of me.

"You good?" He kisses my shoulder.

"So good." There are literally no other words in my brain.

"Me too." He wraps his arms around me. Even though he's still inside me, I have no desire for him to move. "I don't want to say goodbye." His breath tickles my ear as he speaks. "Will you come over to my place for dinner? My chef will already be preparing something."

I snort. His *chef*. I shouldn't be surprised. Karson had someone else to cook for him too. I don't want Leo to take my amusement the wrong way though, so I hasten to add, "That sounds wonderful."

And it does. It makes me wonder whether what's happening between us could lead to something real. It feels life-changing in a good way.

A flash of premonition runs through me and I shiver. It never pays to be too optimistic. I need to remember things have a habit of crashing down. And when the crash comes, I'm not sure I'll be left standing.

8

After a few weeks of dating Camile, I'm beginning to wonder why I spent so long scared of being in a relationship. There's something magical about having a person who wants to hear what happened during my day and snuggle with me on the sofa when I'm tired. Someone to troubleshoot problems with. But my favorite thing is talking about the future. Things like her plans for her designs, which are coming together beautifully, and what I'd like to do after fighting—because let's be real, I'm thirty and won't be able to be a professional fighter forever. I've amassed a small fortune in winnings and sponsorships, which has been invested by someone who knows far more about money than I do, but I don't want to sit back and live off that.

The obvious choice would be to become a coach or a manager, but I don't have the patience for politics. I enjoy MMA, but there's more to me than being an athlete. I've been toying with the idea of starting up a community martial arts program for inner city youth. I know my new teammate, Jase Rawlins, has some experience in that area, and I'm sure he'd give me pointers if I asked. I want to do something that makes a difference and proves I'm a better man than my father. Each day, I'm growing more confident that I am better than him —at least in some regards. I haven't been tempted to do anything that might hurt Camile or screw up what we have. Not even remotely. I love everything about being with her.

"We're here," Camile announces as we pull up outside a networking event hosted by one of my sponsors. It's a yearly opportunity for people to brag about how important they are. I'm contractually required to attend. Considering everything my sponsor has done for me, showing up isn't a hardship. Especially when I get to spend the night with my girl.

I draw her close and press a kiss to the top of her head. "You're stunning."

She's wearing one of the dresses from her new line. It's light purple and brings out the roses in her cheeks. When I look at her, I can hardly breathe because of the way she glows from the inside. It has nothing to do with the dress, nice as it may be. It's all her.

I get out and open the door for Camile, placing a hand on her elbow to help her out of the car. I keep it there while we enter the building. Cameras flash and someone calls my name, but I ignore them. I'm not the biggest celebrity here tonight, so the media won't make too much fuss if they don't get anything printable from me. The moment we enter, Jase's girlfriend, Lena, appears in front of us, her flame-red hair piled elegantly atop her head.

She offers Camile her phone. "Have you seen this?"

Camile scans the screen, her brows knitting together. While the two women aren't exactly friends, they've come to an understanding. Lena is trying not to hold Karson's general assholery against Camile, while Camile has apologized for not noticing the way her brother treated Lena when they were dating.

Camile giggles. "Smitten?"

Lena shrugs. "Well, you two are pretty adorable."

What are they talking about?

I hold out my hand to Camile. "Let me see."

She passes the phone. It's open to a web browser with a tabloid headline entitled "Smitten Kitten: Leo 'The Lion' Delaney Tamed by Love?". I scowl as I read the first few lines.

Professional fighter Leo "The Lion" Delaney, a notoriously slippery bachelor, has been sighted several times with a mystery woman. The curvy bombshell seems to have wrapped Delaney around her finger. Has the lion finally been tamed? Read on for more.

I roll my eyes. "Don't they have anything better to do?"

Lena gives me a look. As a public relations specialist, she knows exactly how much people care about the personal lives of their favorite celebrities and pseudo-celebrities. "At least they haven't tried to dig up any dirt on you."

I nod in acknowledgment. She's right. I should be pleased most media outlets—reputable or not—seem to look on me favorably. The same can't be said for Jase, who'd been in the middle of a media shitstorm when he and Lena met.

"I think it's cute," Cami says.

"Of course you do. They call you a bombshell. That's much better than a fucking kitten." There is no heat in my words. Honestly, I'm relieved no one has insinuated our relationship gives me another potential connection to Karson and the drug scandal.

Camile pings, and Lena and I both stare at her. She's

not carrying a purse and, as far as I can see, isn't holding anything. "Oh, sorry." She colors, and reaches into the folds of her dress, then extracts her phone. "It's just an email."

"Wait, wait, wait." Lena holds up her hands, her tone incredulous. "That dress has pockets?"

"Um, yeah." Camile smooths the fabric to show her a subtle split in the seam, where she's concealed a pocket large enough for a phone and maybe a couple of other items.

"Oh my God. That's amazing. You can't even tell it's there. Where did you get that dress? I need one."

Camile's shoulders straighten and she beams. "It's currently one of a kind. It's one of the designs I've drawn up for my fashion line. The seamstress finished with it last week."

Lena's jaw drops. "Wow. That's seriously impressive." She taps her finger against her chin and a change comes over her. She circles Camile, studying her from different angles. "Have you sold the collection yet?"

"No, but that email is from one of the investors I contacted."

"Open it," Lena insists. "What are you waiting for?"

I wrap an arm around Camile and brush my lips against her temple. "Only if you're comfortable doing that here."

She seems to stop breathing but then nods and returns her attention to her phone. Seconds pass. I don't try to read the screen even though I easily could, because it's up to her to share as much or little as she wants. After a long moment, she squeals and jumps on the spot. Her tits jiggle and I discreetly reach down to adjust myself.

"They want to meet me!"

"Congratulations, baby." I scoop her up in a hug. "I'm so proud of you. When?"

"On Tuesday." Her breathing picks up. "I've only got a couple of days to prepare. Shit."

"You're going to kill it. You're ready for this."

She tilts her head back, slowing down enough to get her bearings. "You're right. I'm completely ready."

"They're going to love you," Lena adds and pulls a business card from her purse. "When they make you an offer, reach out to me at my work number. I have contacts we can use to get you the publicity you deserve."

"Oh, I don't know if I'll be able to afford that kind of thing," Camile stammers.

"You will." Lena is one-hundred-percent confident. "Because any investor worth their salt is going to know you can make them a lot of money with dresses like this."

"Thank you." Camile grins, but then seems to remember something. "I should tell Mom and Dad."

I force myself to keep smiling. I'm glad she's excited to share her good news, but I hope she isn't expecting too much. I haven't met them yet, but from what I can tell, her parents overlook how special she is.

Her mother doesn't respond to Camile's message until we're in the vehicle on the way home, several hours later. Her only comment is "It's a long shot." I grit my teeth because a locked jaw is the only thing that can keep me from insulting the parents of the woman I care about. Why can't they see her for the amazing person she is? But then, I guess they're responsible for raising Karson as well, and if they're anything like him, they're probably blind to accomplishments that aren't sporting. The possibility Karson may have taken after their parents only makes me admire Camile more. She came from the same family, the same background, and yet she's completely different, in the best possible way. That's pretty incredible.

***

CAMILE

I think I'm going to be sick. I duck into the ladies' room attached to the foyer of Barnett Investments, the firm I'm meeting with today, and shut myself in a cubicle. I hover over the toilet bowl until the nausea passes.

My phone rings, and Leo's name pops up on the screen. I cringe. I left him in the foyer while I made my impromptu dash for somewhere safe to puke. He's supposed to be training today but said being here with me was more important. Not that he'll be coming into the meeting. I'll do that on my own. I ignore the call, leave the cubicle, and check myself in the mirror. Smart powder blue blazer, delicate pink top, black pants. I'm dressed for success, all in items of my own design.

"You can do this," I tell my reflection. "You. Have. Got. This." I leave the ladies' room and give Leo a sheepish smile as I emerge into the foyer. "Sorry about that."

"Are you all right?"

"Yeah." I take the manila folder from him and tuck it under my arm.

"I'll be right here." He kisses me. "Go kick some ass."

"I will."

I stride to the reception desk and tell the receptionist my name. Within minutes, I'm escorted to the elevator and led through an open office to a conference room. Inside, two women and one man are already seated. They look up as I enter.

"Camile." One of the women stands and extends a

hand. She's elegantly attired, Black, and somewhere in her forties. "I'm Renita Brady. These are my colleagues, Simon Farrell and Dana Stone. Thank you for coming."

"Thank you for agreeing to meet with me." I lower myself into the only available seat and reach for the glass of water I assume is meant for me. I take a sip because suddenly my throat is parched, then I set the folder down and open it to the first page. I've practiced my presentation nearly a dozen times, but being here in front of them is different from saying it in front of Leo and Lena.

"We were impressed by what you sent through," Dana says. "Feel free to start wherever you like, and if we have questions, we'll cut in. How's that sound?"

"Good." I pause for a moment and then all the words I've rehearsed pour from me without any conscious thought. I have no idea exactly what I'm saying, but they nod and exchange glances so it seems to be going well. Finally, they begin asking questions. To my surprise, few of them are about the designs. Simon asks about sourcing materials. He jots notes as I stumble through a reply. I've looked into sourcing and costing, but the way he studies me over his glasses makes me feel like a kid who forgot to do her homework.

Meanwhile, Dana wants to know how deeply I've researched what would be needed to launch the collection, and Renita queries my decision to pitch to them rather than directly to a company. Eventually, they ask me to leave the room while they confer. I wait outside, nerves rioting in my stomach. My palms are clammy and my breath comes in short pants. I can't believe I actually did it. Even if nothing comes of this meeting, I'm so proud I was able to get through a pitch to investors without making a fool of myself. How many people could say that?

While I'm sitting on the chair outside the meeting room, my phone buzzes. I check it, assuming it's Leo, but my eyebrows draw together at the sight of an altogether different name: Karson.

Karson: *Tell me you aren't dating that preachy asshole Delaney.*

I scowl. I hear nothing from him for ages, and now he wants to butt into my love life? I don't think so.

Camile: *Yes, I am. He's a really good guy.*

It doesn't take long for Karson to reply.

Karson: *If I'd known you wanted to fuck a fighter, I'd have made sure you had a better option. Delaney is a sanctimonious prick.*

I roll my eyes. When my brother pulls out the big words, it means he's really pissed off. Strangely, I don't care. I'm over his bullshit. Completely and totally over it.

Camile: *You don't actually have any say in who I date. I'm with Leo. We're together. Deal with it.*

At that moment, Dana appears in the doorway and waves me back into the conference room. I put my phone away and ignore the buzzes as it starts to ring. I've said my piece. Now it's up to him to decide if he can handle it.

I return to the same chair I'd previously occupied and keep my feet planted firmly on the ground. I'm so sweaty I could slip off the seat if I'm not careful.

Simon plucks the cap from his fancy pen and then clicks it back into place. "Thank you, Camile. We appreciate you taking time out of your day to speak to us."

My heart sinks. He's going to brush me off, I just know it. That's the beginning of a "sorry, but" talk.

"...and we'd be pleased to offer you enough funding to launch your collection and manufacture a limited run of each item, with future funding contingent on sales numbers."

I blink at him, uncomprehending.

He takes off his glasses and smiles. "We'd like to invest in you. Congratulations."

Oh my God.

My jaw drops and I gape at him. Can this really be happening? "Thank you. Thank you so much. I promise you won't regret it."

"Here." Renita passes me a piece of paper with several numbers scrawled on it. They're big enough that when I read them, I struggle to haul in a breath. "We'll need to do some additional analysis, but this is our estimate for what we can offer you. We also have a mentoring program we think you'd benefit from, where one of our project managers can work with you to build your general business knowledge."

"That would be amazing." I can hardly process it.

"We'll come back to you with an official contract that your lawyer can review. In the meantime, go and celebrate. You're about to become somebody to watch in women's fashion."

I thank them all profusely, then Dana escorts me out of the conference room and back to the elevator. I squeal as soon as the doors close and I'm finally alone.

They said yes!

Holy crap. I'm going to be a professional fashion designer with a show and everything. I shake my head and then can't stop shaking it because it's all so surreal. When I step into the foyer, Leo catches sight of my shaking head and his face falls. Realizing he's misunderstood, I launch myself into his arms. He catches me and holds me tight.

"They made me an offer," I whisper. "My dream is coming true."

He kisses me, and my heart feels like it might explode from an overload of joy. Not only are my career dreams becoming a reality, but my emotional ones are too. I'm falling in love with Leo Delaney, and based on the way his eyes soften as he gazes at me, he feels the same.

"I'm so happy for you." He pulls me into another kiss —this one a bit too hot and heavy to be appropriate for the foyer of a reputable business. "Let's go home and celebrate." He winks. "Naked."

9

———

Weeks later, I'm practicing Jiu-Jitsu with Jimmy when I notice Enya hovering over us. I flip the kid over and clamber off him. Jiu-Jitsu is skill-based, and being bigger doesn't necessarily mean being better, but with the level of body mass difference between Jimmy and me, he doesn't stand much chance of coming out on top. He's not scrawny, but he's all lean muscle while I've got brawn.

"What's going on?" I ask Enya as I roll onto my butt and look up at her.

She dithers for a moment, which is unlike her. She may not always be as aggressive as Seth's sister, Harley, but she's direct. "I just wanted to say I'm sorry for what's happening with Cami's show. I wasn't sure whether to mention it or not, since it might be a sore point. Is she doing okay?"

Lead sinks to the bottom of my stomach. "What do you mean?"

Her eyebrows knit together. "The influencer. You don't know?"

I scramble to my feet and put my hands on my hips. "Know what?"

She pulls a face. "Some asshole on social media is calling for people to boycott the show because Cami is the sister of a drug cheat." She hesitates, then adds, "And he insinuates she's probably dating another one. He's calling her designs 'junkie chic.'"

I try to swallow but my throat feels thick. Shame bubbles in my gut. I'd worried people might view my connection with Camile as another reason to doubt my innocence in the City Fight Center drug scandal, but it never occurred to me I could taint her in the same way. Fuck, I'm self-centered. I encouraged her to reach for her dreams, and now I might be the reason they're snatched away. I only hope nobody approaches Karson for a comment because after how I told him to fuck off when he confronted me about dating his sister, he might say something spiteful just to mess with us. He's vindictive like that.

"Does this influencer guy have many followers?"

"I wish I could say not, but he does. He's a bit of an extremist, and you know how those types are. Their fans are die-hard loyalists."

"That's messed up," Jimmy grouses. "People shouldn't talk shit when they don't know anything about it."

"I have to go."

I hurry to the locker where I keep my phone during training and grab it. A quick Google search leads me to several hits. I click the top one and scan the text. My stomach rolls uncomfortably. Has Camile seen this? It will devastate her. Hell, it's devastating *me*. I've been starting to think she and I can make things work long-term, and that I won't hurt her the way Dad did to Mom, but perhaps this is how I bring her down. It's not the same, but that doesn't make it less of a problem. I pocket the phone and snatch the rest of my belongings, then knock on Seth's office door. I wait for him to respond. I learned the hard way not to barge in, in case he's with Ashlin.

"Come in."

I stick my head around the door. "I need to leave. Something has come up."

He nods. "You done everything you have to?"

"Not weights yet, but I'll use my own at home."

"You'd better. I've nearly got this fight with Ricky locked in."

"Great." I should be more enthusiastic, considering how badly I've wanted that fight, but I'm too preoccupied by thoughts of Camile. "Keep me updated."

"Will do."

"See you." I nod in parting and dodge out the side exit. My mind races as I make my way to my car. The drive to Camile's apartment—where she's been working during the day since she finished with her previous job—seems to take forever. Finally, I park in the underground lot, get one of the neighbors to buzz me in, and take the stairs to her level. I pause in the corridor outside, wondering how I want to play this. If she knows what's good for her, she'll put some distance between us in the lead-up to the show, and the thought of that makes me want to scream. It's so fucking unfair. Neither of us had anything to do with her brother's mess and yet, we're both paying the price. In all my worrying about what might go wrong, I never foresaw this.

"Leo?" I turn and find her standing behind me, the key to the apartment clutched in her hand. "Shouldn't you still be at the gym?"

"There's something I need to tell you."

"Oh." She stiffens. "What?"

I gesture toward the door. "Maybe you should go in and sit down."

Her mouth tightens. "You're freaking me out. What is it?"

Reaching over, I take the key from her and slot it into the lock, then I place my palm on her lower back and guide her in. We sit side by side on the sofa, and I clasp her hand in mine. God, I wish I didn't have to be the one to break the news.

"Some asshole online is calling your designs junkie chic and asking people to boycott your show because of me and Karson."

Her expression doesn't change, and that's when I realize: she already knows. What the hell?

"He's a sports guy," she says. "His following doesn't overlap much with my target audience."

How can she be so calm about this?

"But what if his message spreads? What if he has connections?"

"Then we'll deal with whatever happens, but at the moment, nothing has."

I pinch the bridge of my nose. "I'm so sorry, Cami. This is all my fault."

"No, it's not." She gently removes my hand from my face so she can look at me. "It's Karson's fault. He's the one who made both of us look dirty. This isn't on you."

I press my lips together, knowing she's technically correct, but in my soul, I feel responsible. I always knew I'd hurt her somehow. And it's occurred to me before that we have the potential to damage each other's reputations. I just figured her connection to Karson would end up impacting mine, and I was prepared to take the risk. I didn't expect it to happen the other way around.

"Why didn't you mention it?" I ask.

"Because I knew you'd react this way." She waves a hand up and down my body as if to say "case in point." "But it's not a big deal, and making it one just gives that loser more credit than he deserves. Don't let it get to you."

I clench my teeth. All the well-meaning platitudes in the world won't undo the damage he might have already done. But we can get out in front of it and do damage control. "Would it help if we made a public announcement that I'm not affiliated with your fashion line? Maybe I need to keep a low profile so people realize you're more than just an extension of Karson or me. Whatever we need to do, tell me." I hate feeling helpless. "Even if it means I can't come to the show. I'll stay away to protect you."

Camile flinches and her eyes shine with reproach. Damn, I'm already hurting her and all I'm trying to do is make it better.

***

I can't believe Leo would even consider not coming to my first fashion show. Especially when he's the reason it's happening. Without him, I can't be certain I'd have had the guts to approach investors in the first place.

"You're coming," I tell him, not allowing a smidgen of uncertainty into my voice. "I've had a lifetime of people overlooking me or not being there for me, and I refuse to let you be one of them."

His face falls. "Baby, I promise, that's not what it's about."

I raise my chin and fight really hard not to waver. "I want you to come. My parents are never going to be as supportive as I'd like, but having you on my team for the past few weeks has meant everything." I rub my chest, feeling an ache deep within it. "I'm falling for you, Leo, and that's more important than whether a handful of people boycott my event out of some misguided sense of justice." When something dark flickers across his expression, I add an entreaty. "Isn't it?"

He softens. "Of course." His arm wraps around my shoulders and he draws me close. I lean into his strong chest and enjoy how protected he makes me feel. He's so big. So solid. And so very sexy. "It's just not right. People shouldn't be able to act as judge, jury, and executioner with no proof."

I sigh. Honestly, the influencer's crusade bothers me too, but Lena has already promised to balance it out with some positive articles, and other than that, there's nothing we can do, so there's no point in stressing. "That's how the court of public opinion works."

He kisses my forehead. "It sucks."

I giggle because he's not wrong. "I know. But please don't let it keep you away from the show. I need your support."

"Okay," he murmurs, but his brow is furrowed, and I know he's still mulling it over. I'm getting better at figuring out when his brain is stuck on a hamster wheel because he gets this annoyed, faraway look. "Whatever you need, baby."

I smooth my thumb over his forehead. "Everything will be okay."

The crinkle forms again almost immediately. "I guess we'll have to wait and see."

Sensing that's the best I'm going to get out of him for now, I press my lips to his and tease my tongue along the seam of his mouth. He groans and grasps my face so he can deepen the kiss.

"I want you so bad," I murmur. Over the past few weeks with Leo, I've grown more comfortable with my sexuality. He's proven he likes me as I am in every way that matters.

"Same." He groans as I reach between us and cup his cock. "God, yes. More."

I rub the growing bulge his shorts don't do much to contain. When his breathing becomes ragged, I slip my hand beneath the waistband and into his briefs. I fist his cock and stroke it slowly enough that his hips jerk, seeking more.

His eyes find mine. They're dark with desperation. "Please, Cami. Need you."

Yes. I love the way this man makes me feel. I'm already wet for him, and desire soaks my panties as I watch him struggle to take what I'm giving without overpowering me. He's riding the edge of control. My favorite place for him to be. I release his cock and it thumps against his belly, smearing precum on his shirt. He throws his head back and curses. But before he has time to make demands, I lift my skirt, shove my ruined panties to the side, and straddle him.

"Fuck." He grips my thighs and shifts me into place above his throbbing dick. I encircle it with my fingers and guide myself, sinking onto him inch by inch as he fills me. We've been going without condoms for a few days now because we're both free of STIs and I'm taking protection, but the sensation still overwhelms me. A shudder racks my body. He's so hard and hot. I can feel each pulse as he fights to hold on to control.

I whimper. "I'm so full of you."

"You're so tight, baby." His voice is soft but strained. "So goddamn snug. Like your pussy was made for me."

I place my hands on his chest and ride him, working myself up and down his cock, feeling the drag of his thick shaft against my clit. Every time he bottoms out inside me, I feel like he's touching my heart. I watch his face, enthralled by the harsh lines and shadows.

"That's it," he murmurs, reaching between us to thumb my clit. "Take what you need."

Sensation winds tighter and tighter within me. My body draws taut like a bow string. I work my hips faster and capture his mouth for an intense kiss.

"I'm going to—Oh God!"

"Yeah." His fingertips sink deeper into my hips. "Come on my cock. It's the only cock you're ever going to come on again."

His possessive words send me careening over a precipice. My channel flutters around him, and I scream as an orgasm consumes me. He thrusts furiously and then stiffens and grits out my name. I feel liquid heat scorching my insides and shiver in the knowledge that he's branded me as his.

I am his.

Every part of me belongs to Leo Delaney.

But I belong to myself too. Because even as I lie panting against his chest, cracks are appearing in the blissful world we've been building. I clutch him and pray our relationship won't crumble. But if it does, I'll survive, because I finally know who I am, and that woman is strong and capable. I'm never going back to the woman I used to be.

10

Leo

It's the day of Camile's fashion show, and I should be at home choosing a suit so I look good on her arm. Instead, I'm at the gym, pounding the crap out of a bag because no matter how much she says she wants me there, I can't help feeling like I'll hurt her if I go. It's *her* day. It should be all about her. That online influencer asshole hasn't let up, and if I stand at Camile's side, where I want to be, people might make it all about me rather than her. She's had enough of that kind of shit to deal with from her brother without me contributing to it. Perhaps I can sneak in the back so I'm there for her but not in the spotlight. If I call, I can let her know I haven't stood her up. Wouldn't that be the best of both worlds?

Damn, I wish I had someone to talk to about this. When I was younger, I used to go to my dad for advice, but that stopped the moment I caught him with another woman. I replaced him with Stan, my coach, who turned out to also be crooked. Fuck them both. The thought of Dad sours my mood even further. I've been thinking of him too much lately. Of how he played with Mom's emotions over and over again. I've already hurt Camile once. I don't know how best to avoid repeating it.

"Hey."

I flinch at the sound of a voice behind me. I'd thought I was alone. But Seth is standing behind me, arms crossed over his chest.

"Shouldn't you be getting ready for the show?" He's wearing a tux that fits well, but he doesn't seem comfortable in it. I get the impression he'd like to rip it off Superman style. "The girls are already there. They wanted to be early so they could get seats in the front, where Cami would be able to see her support team."

"I don't know what to do," I admit. "She's worked so hard for this, and all of the attention should be on her and her designs. If I turn up, I'm worried it'll turn into a gossip-fest instead. She deserves better than that."

Seth nods. "I'm sure it's not easy to have a famous brother and a famous boyfriend."

I shift from one foot to the other, eager to hit something again. His eyes follow the movement, but he doesn't back off. Then again, Iron-Shin Seth Isles doesn't back down from anything. Except, perhaps, an angry Ashlin.

"What would you do?" I ask.

He rubs his bristled jaw. "If it were Ash?"

"Yeah."

He cocks his head. "Depends. What does she want?"

"Theoretically, she wants you there."

"Hmm." He doesn't say anything more. I want to growl at him to hurry up but that won't do any good. He'll speak when he's ready. "And it's supposed to be all about her, right?"

"Yes." I bite back my impatience. Why is he asking questions he already knows the answers to?

He cracks a smile. "Well, if it's all about what makes her happy, and she wants me there, then I'd go. End of story."

"It's not that black and white. What if my being there screws everything up?"

Seth shakes his head. "You're making it more complicated than it needs to be. The only question you should be asking yourself is whether you're prepared to deal a massive blow to Cami's heart by not being there when she needs you. You're considering doing something that will definitely hurt her just because you're worried about something that *might* hurt her. I know you have some issues with your dad, but you're not him, and Cami isn't weak. You need to trust her when she tells you what she wants. Some asshole online, who she doesn't give a shit about, can't wound her the way you can."

"Fuck." He's right. The realization is a full-body experience. It warms my insides and loosens my muscles. Camile says she wants me there, so that's where I need to be.

I'm *not* my father.

I may look like him. I may even fight like him. But I'm not him, and I'm not doomed to repeat his mistakes. I've forged my own path in my career, and it's time I do the same for my relationship.

"I need to go." I race toward the exit.

"Good choice," he calls after me. "See you there."

I cross the parking lot and press the button to unlock my car, then I fling myself into the driver's seat and shove the key into the ignition. I still have plenty of time to get there, but I want to make sure she knows I'm by her side. She has enough to worry about without me being MIA. I should have got my head out of my ass and realized that sooner.

I drive back to my place, shower, and grab my nicest suit from the closet. Barely ten minutes later, I'm heading across town, but I seem to hit every goddamn red light in the city. Then, impulsively, I pull over and dash into a flower shop. I clearly have no idea what I'm doing, but the florist takes pity on me and helps out.

Finally, I'm back on the road, but when police lights flash ahead and the traffic slows to a stop, my stomach sinks. Looks like there's been a crash. Thankfully not a terrible one, but it might be enough to make me late.

I just hope I make it before the show opens. I'll never forgive myself if I don't.

Camile

He's not here.

The show begins in five minutes, and there's still no sign of Leo. I glance at my phone to see if he's called, but there's nothing other than a message from a while ago telling me he was on his way. He said he'd be here by now. An insecure little voice in the back of my mind whispers he's not coming.

I'm standing in the wings of the stage, watching while the emcee prepares for her introductory talk. She'll be opening the show and keeping everything running smoothly. Then, at the end, she'll invite me to say a few words. That's the part I'm most nervous about. Everyone will have already seen my designs and either loved them or hated them. I'll have to stand in front of them and welcome their judgment.

"You've got this," I murmur to myself. "They're going to love you."

"Damn right they will," Lena agrees.

I smile as she approaches. Despite our differences, she's been an absolute godsend while I've been planning this event. She's dealt with all the media releases and helped guide me to where I need to be. I can't help but hope this is the start of a friendship with her. It certainly feels that way, and I'm so grateful to have a strong woman in my corner. "Thank you for everything you've done. I couldn't have pulled this off without you."

"You're welcome." She winks. "It's going to be awesome." She gives me a little wave as she heads to take care of whatever the next thing is on her to-do list. Meanwhile, I've done everything I can prior to starting, so I stay where I am and wait. But then my phone rings and my heart leaps in response. I withdraw it, hoping like hell it's Leo, but the hope dies a swift death when I see Caller ID. It's Mom. I debate whether to answer. I called ages ago to tell her and Dad about the show. For a few minutes, it had seemed like she might be proud of me, but when she'd heard my clothing collection was for plus-size women, she'd dismissed it. Apparently I can't be considered a success in her eyes until I'm designing outfits for women with a size zero waist. The problem is, I have no interest in that. There are enough designers out there for smaller women, whereas I'm helping those who don't always get the chance to feel beautiful. Maybe it's not what she'd like, but it matters to me. I glance at the emcee and see she's still fixing her outfit, so I assume I have a few minutes before we're live. I answer the call.

"Hi, Mom."

"Hello, Camile." Her voice is polite but detached. "Karson seems more sullen than usual tonight. Would you be able to speak to him? You always have such a way of getting through to him."

I shake my head, hardly able to believe what I'm hearing. "No, Mom. I can't. My fashion show is about to start. Honestly, that's probably what he's upset about. For once, everything isn't about him." My brother and I have spoken a couple of times since I told him about Leo. He hasn't come around, but he seems to have accepted he can't push me into ending the relationship, so at least that's something. More than I expected, to tell the truth.

"Oh, the show is tonight?" To her credit, she sounds genuinely interested. "Is it too late to get a ticket and come along?"

My mouth opens and closes. I don't know how to respond. It's the first time she's ever offered me even the slightest hint of the support she's shown Karson over the years. Part of me wants to lap it up, but she had the chance to reserve a ticket when I first told her about the show and she didn't do it. So does she really want to be here, or is it just that she hasn't had any better offers tonight? Either way, the event is sold out thanks to some solid publicity from Lena's firm.

"I'm sorry, but there aren't any tickets left." I swallow to moisten my dry throat. "If you'd wanted to come, you should have said when I asked."

"Oh, honey. I didn't know what my plans were going to be."

"But you managed to make time for almost every one of Karson's fights," I remind her. "Because you prioritized him." I take a deep breath and prepare to say what I've needed to for a really long time. "That's what I want. To be prioritized. I'm doing what I love, and I'm going to succeed with or without your support. I'd really like to share my happiness with you, but whether or not that happens is entirely your choice." I soften my tone. "Perhaps we can get in early to save you a ticket for the next show." Because there will be another one, I'm certain of it.

Mom is quiet for so long I begin to wonder if she's hung up, but then she speaks. "I'm sorry if I've made you feel like you're not a priority." Surprisingly, her voice is heavy. She seems to have taken my words to heart. "You've always been so self-contained. You never seemed to need our encouragement. Karson thrived on the attention, so I suppose we showered it on him at your expense." She pauses, then adds, "When the next show is on, I'd really like to come. But I'll buy a ticket, just like your father and I always did for Karson's fights. I want to support you with our money, not just our presence."

"That's not necessary," I protest, even as my heart fills with warmth at the gesture.

"I insist." I can tell she won't be swayed. "Now, go enjoy your show. Congratulations, Camile. Maybe I could come over for brunch tomorrow so we can talk?"

I smile and nod. "I'd like that. I'll see you then."

"Goodbye."

As I end the call, music begins to play. I'm oddly calm as the emcee strides to the center of the stage and greets the audience. I peer out at them as much as I can while remaining hidden. Most people in attendance are women, although I see a few men scattered throughout. The emcee speaks into the microphone, but I can't make out her words. She talks for several minutes and then leaves the stage. A song comes over the loudspeakers, and one of the models sashays onto the catwalk, wearing a fabulous evening gown.

"Cami." Arms wrap around me from behind and Leo's woodsy, masculine scent fills my nostrils. A bouquet appears in front of me, clasped in his hands. "I'm so sorry I'm late." He presses a kiss to the top of my head. "There was a car accident and I got rerouted. Then, when I arrived, the paparazzi swarmed. I don't know what Lena did, but they're like ravenous wolves out there."

I relax into him. "I'm just glad you're here."

Thank God, I don't have to do this alone. Today might be my time to shine, but it wouldn't mean anything without someone to share it with. I turn just enough to press a kiss to his lips, then I place the flowers aside and settle against his body to watch the show. It's a whirl of color, beautiful women, and all-out magic. I'm pleased I hired an event manager because it means I can enjoy my moment without having to troubleshoot every little issue that comes up. Plus, with Leo at my back, I have absolutely no desire to move.

His breath stirs the hair beside my ear. "I love you, Cami."

I press a hand to my mouth, and happy tears fill my eyes as my heart overflows. Now, this evening is perfect. "I love you too." I tilt my face so I can see him. "Even if you were late."

He nips my mouth. "I'll make it up to you a thousand times over as long as you keep loving me."

"I will." I know beyond a shadow of a doubt that I'll feel this way about him forever. Nobody else has ever lit up my life the way he does.

We kiss. Softly at first, but the heat between us grows until we're making out like giddy teenagers. I don't know how long we stay that way, but the clearing of a throat drags me back to the present. The event planner is standing in front of me, grinning mischievously.

"Time to take a bow," she says.

"Really?" That went fast.

She gestures for me to step onto the stage. Leo steps back and I take a deep breath and stride onto the stage. When I reach the center, I sweep into a deep bow. I straighten, and the emcee hands me the microphone. I freeze for a few seconds, paralyzed by the faces swimming in front of me, but then Leo appears at my side and squeezes my hand, reminding me where I am.

"Thank you, everyone, for coming," I say, managing to pick out Tony's face in the crowd. Enya is beside him, and I speak directly to her, both as a way to soothe my nerves and because I hope she understands how much her support means to me. Like Leo, she refuses to let me downplay myself, and thanks to her, I finally feel like I can cross off that third item on my list—*make a friend.*

"This show is a dream come true for me, and I'm so glad you took the time to be here tonight. I'd like to thank the team who made this possible. I won't mention you all by name, but you know who you are, and I think you're wonderful." I smile up at Leo. "My handsome other half has been behind me, encouraging me the whole time." His expression softens and he mouths "Love you." I turn back to the audience. "I hope you've enjoyed yourselves. If you spotted any designs you simply must have, there's an order center in the back right corner of the hall." I gesture to it. "Or you can order online at Camile Couture dot com. Have a lovely rest of your evening."

I hand the microphone back to the emcee. Leo and I walk hand-in-hand off the stage. He draws me into a corner away from everyone else and pins me to the wall.

"I want a private viewing of the collection since somebody distracted me from the show."

Excitement fizzes throughout my body, and my nerve endings come alive in each place he touches. "That can be arranged. But the models might not be available."

He rubs the tip of his nose against mine. "There's only one woman I'm interested in stripping those outfits off."

My breath stutters as he lays a hand possessively on my hip. "Two hours," I say. "Then we can get out of here."

He smiles so tenderly it makes me weak in the knees. "No way in hell are we rushing away. Not when you've worked so hard for this. I can wait however long it takes."

"Just remember you said that." I kiss him once more. "Because I'm going to be obsessively checking orders all night." If I hit the right threshold, my investors have promised enough capital to open my own designer boutique. Although if the orders go well enough, I might not need their contribution."

"I'm not going anywhere," he says. "You can bask in your glory all you fucking want. You deserve it."

I wrap my arms around him and hold him tight. He's right. I *do* deserve it. And even if my family aren't here and some people will always think poorly of me, I have Leo, and he's all the family I need.

EPILOGUE

JIMMY

A parade of hot women in front of me all night, and
the only one I'm interested in doesn't realize I exist
except as a little brother figure. Enya Sears, the leading
lady in my fantasies of relationship bliss, claps loudly as
Camile takes a final bow and leaves the stage on Leo's
arm. I bet they'll be getting it on tonight. Meanwhile, I'll
be alone in my cold bed, reliving tonight's events over
and over and playing out a dozen what-might-have-
happened-if scenarios in my mind.

What might have happened if I'd reached over and
put a hand on her thigh?

What might have happened if I'd been brave enough
to go in for a kiss as we left?

What might have happened if I'd finally gotten the
guts to tell her how I feel and ask her on a date?

Hell, I don't know why one woman scares me so
much. I can take punches to the face seven days a week,
but put me in close proximity to Enya and my brain
shuts down. Maybe it's because I've had a crush on her
since I was eighteen and saw her on television at a pay-

per-view fight event. She'd looked like the kind of cute college girl I'd imagined meeting when I left school, but then she'd downed her opponent with a perfectly executed roundhouse kick and I was a goner.

"I'm so glad it went well," Enya says as the applause tapers off. "I might see if I can catch Cami and then head home for bed. I'm beat."

"Me too."

She gives me a skeptical look, like she expects me to be out partying into the wee hours of the morning. But although I've done my fair share of that in the past, I haven't been with anyone since she transferred to our gym a few months ago. I knew as soon as I met her I'd be celibate until I figured out how to make a move. I don't want her to see me with anyone else, nor give her reason to wonder if I'm capable of being faithful. With her, I'd be in, one hundred percent. Even if I haven't told her that yet.

Her phone buzzes. She checks it and scowls.

"What's up?" Tony asks from her other side.

"Ugh." She makes a face. "My family are threatening to set me up on a blind date for my sister's wedding. They think there's something wrong with me because I'm single."

"There's nothing wrong with you," I snap.

Tony smirks, and I curse myself for being so obvious. I'm pretty sure the guys all know how I feel about Enya. The only one who doesn't is her.

"Thanks." She smiles, but her expression is weary. I want to hug her better, but I don't think she'd welcome it. "I only hope they choose better this time."

"Wait." I hold up a finger. "They've set you up on a blind date before?"

She nods. "Last year. When I went home for my

birthday. He was a nice guy, but we had absolutely nothing in common."

When she'd first mentioned the blind date, I'd halfway thought she was joking, but she's serious. My insides knot together. I can't sit back and watch her be set up with someone else. Not if there's even the faintest chance they might hit it off. Which means I need to do something and do it soon.

I only hope she doesn't break my heart.

BONUS EPILOGUE

Leo - Six months later

I dodge a blow thrown by a man who's both my opponent and teammate—Gabe "The Mind Reader" Mendoza. Even though this is technically an exhibition fight to raise money for charity, and there will be no winner, I'm a little skittish because he knocked me out when we fought for the Ruby Knuckles championship. I'd rather not run the risk of history repeating. Fortunately, Gabe is as experienced as I am and he knows his own power, which means that while he's not being gentle as a kitten, he's not going to do any real damage either. I trust him, and he trusts me. But that doesn't mean there isn't a little friendly competition between us.

I circle around and test his defenses, looking for an opportunity to strike. He quickly lifts his foot as though he's about to kick, but I don't react. He's good at faking action and then taking advantage of his opponent's reaction. That's how I ended up getting dropped last time. I push kick him in the stomach and the audience roars. It isn't a big hit, but it's better than nothing. He beckons with his gloved hand and I crook an eyebrow. I'm not running into any of his traps.

But then Seth yells at us to move. The crowd wants action. I explode forward and take Gabe to the ground. We roll, battling for dominance, until the timer ends the round. We stand and bump gloves, then retreat to our respective sides of the cage. Neither of us have our usual people in the corner today. Enya is standing in mine and Devon is covering Gabe because Seth didn't want it to look like he was playing favorites.

"You're doing good," Enya says as Tony rests an ice pack on my upper back. "But you're holding back too much. The audience wants more bang for their buck. Got it?"

I nod.

Someone passes Enya a water bottle, and she gestures for me to open my mouth so she can squirt it in. I swallow, feeling water run down my chin. Just as I'm about to refocus on Enya, I catch sight of a flash of color and groan. *Fucking hell.* It's Camile, circling the cage in a tiny denim skirt and a corset-style top I've seen among her latest series of designs. My gaze lingers on her, and she catches my eye and gives me a saucy smile. She puts a little shimmy in her hips as she passes by, and my mouth feels dry again despite the water.

Fuck. Every lucky asshole here can see her shapely legs and the shadow between her beautiful tits. Not to mention the other curves of her unreasonably curvy body. Who's responsible for this? I'm going to bloody their nose for real once I get out of the cage.

I narrow my eyes at Enya. "Did you know about that?"

She shakes her head. "You think I would have gone along with it if I did? I love her to bits, but she's a distraction."

Maybe. But she's the sexiest fucking distraction I've ever seen.

A bell signals for the seconds to get out of the cage. Enya hops out and Tony removes the ice from my back, then I step into the center with Gabe. He jerks his forehead toward the gate Camile just exited through and winks. The bastard. He wouldn't like it if Sydney were the one parading around in next to nothing.

"Good promotion for her designs," he calls around his mouth guard. "Plus, she thought that seeing her might motivate you to kick my ass."

I scowl but don't respond as the action starts again. The next few minutes pass in a blur of fists, feet, and throws. I have renewed vigor and Gabe seems to be enjoying the change of pace. By the time we finish, I'm dripping sweat.

"You just wait," I say as I tear out my mouth guard. "Next time, it'll be your girl getting lusted over by hundreds of random men."

His expression darkens, but then he shakes his head. "No, I don't think so. Yours has a clothing line. Mine doesn't. Sorry, but you'll have to get used to it."

I narrow my eyes. But then, right on time, Seth appears and offers me a microphone and the box I asked him to hold earlier. I tap the microphone to make sure it's working, then speak into it.

"Cami, could you join me?" I squint against the lights, scanning the room for her. Finally, I see her hurrying toward me, a confused furrow on her brow.

"What are you doing?" she hisses as she reaches me.

In answer, I drop onto one knee. Bursts of color bloom on her cheeks.

"Camile Hayes, you are the most talented, loving, wonderful woman I know, and I'm proud to call you mine. These past few months have been the happiest of my life. I love watching you spread your wings. You make me a better man." I glance out at our audience, who seem to be waiting with bated breath. "My love for you isn't quiet; it rages like a storm and I want everyone to know how incredible you are. Will you marry me?"

"Yes." She grabs my hand and pulls me to my feet, then wraps her arms around me so tightly I can feel her entire body tremble. "I love you."

I hold her close, ignoring the fact I'm sweaty. As long as she doesn't mind, I don't either. When she draws back, I offer her the ring box. She gasps when she sets eyes on the funky diamond ring Lena helped me choose.

"It's perfect." She slots it onto her finger. Primal satisfaction swells within me at the sight, but I resist the urge to beat on my chest. The roar of applause almost deafens me.

I thread my fingers through Camile's and kiss the back of her hand. "It's you and me now, baby. There's no getting rid of me." I will always be by her side. I kissed any doubts goodbye months ago and haven't looked back. She makes me happy, and in return, I'll make it my life's mission to do the same for her.

She smiles in a way that touches every hidden corner of my heart. "As if I'd want to. You're my smitten kitten, and I'll never forget it."

I sigh. She'll never let go of that moniker. But as long as we're together, she can call me whatever the hell she wants. "Come on, fiancé. What say we get out of here?"

Hands joined, we leave the cage, heading toward our future, and it's so damn bright.

THE END

FIGHTER'S FAKE OUT EXCERPT

Jimmy

The moment I step outside the MMA gym where I train as a professional fighter, I hear someone talking. I'm sweating like crazy from the workout my coach put me through, and my heart is pounding in my ears, but I recognize the voice.

Enya.

I could probably be blindfolded underwater and still know Enya's voice when I hear it. I had a crush on the woman long before I ever met her, but since we started training together, my feelings have spiraled out of control. Not that she knows I exist, except as some kind of younger brother figure. Because that's just my fucking luck.

But I've never heard her like this. She sounds stressed. Unhappy. I hesitate by the corner of the building, not wanting to interrupt. Unfortunately, she's standing between me and my car, which is parked in the lot adjoining Crown MMA—the premier facility for training professional MMA fighters in Las Vegas.

"Please don't," she begs. "The last thing I need is to

spend the weekend of Emma's wedding trying to juggle five blind dates just so you guys can settle a bet. You know how much I hate when you set me up."

My jaw firms. This again. Enya previously mentioned her sister is trying to arrange a blind date for when she visits Wisconsin. The idea of her spending time with one man is bad enough, but five? If I have to sit on the sidelines while that happens, I'll go fucking insane.

"I don't care if you think your guy is perfect for me. I'm asking you to drop this and make sure the others do too."

I wince. If there's anything I hate, it's Enya being distressed. I've been mulling over her blind date situation since she first told me about it. Maybe it's time to man up and do something about my crush. I can't continue this way forever.

Straightening my shoulders, I round the corner and find Enya with one hand on her hip, the other pressing a phone to her ear. My insides tremble, but I march up to her and hold out a hand. "Give me the phone."

She shakes her head and tries to wave me away.

"Please," I persist.

She cocks her head. "Hang on a sec, Kels."

She passes me the phone.

I raise it to my ear. "Enya will call you back in a moment."

Then I hang up.

Enya's mouth drops open. "What the hell?" she demands. "That was my sister!"

"I don't care who it was. She was upsetting you."

"So you hung up on her?" She jabs me in the chest with a finger. "You can't just do that."

I try to ignore the angry flash of her gorgeous brown eyes and the adorable tilt of her upturned nose.

If I let myself stare at her, I'll forget what I want to say, and that will get me nowhere fast. "You need a date for your sister's wedding."

She rolls her eyes. "It seems I already have five of them. Have you decided to get on the bandwagon and set me up with one of your friends too?"

"God no." I shudder at the thought. "I'm offering myself as an alternative. Tell Kelsey that you can't do any blind dates because you're already bringing someone. *Me.*"

For a long moment, she doesn't respond and I think she's considering the possibility. But then she laughs. Fucking *laughs*. Discomfort prickles across my skin, but I don't rescind the offer. I've finally grown a set of balls, and I refuse to back down.

"You can't seriously want to spend an entire weekend with my crazy family just to save me from the awkwardness of a few blind dates."

I relax, relieved her laughter has nothing to do with me. I already know she's a million miles out of my league, and I'd been scared she might tell me so to my face. Not that she's cruel enough to do that, but fear isn't always logical. I cross my arms and give her a look. "Can and do. It's win-win. You get to avoid a fuckton of awkwardness and I get a trip to Wisconsin."

She scoffs. "Yeah, because Wisconsin is everybody's idea of a great holiday destination."

I shrug. "Could be worse. I've never been before."

In fact, I've never been out of Nevada, but I don't feel like admitting that. She's competed in Europe, Australia, and the United Kingdom. Compared to her, I've led a very sheltered life.

"You know my family live on a farm, right?" She sounds skeptical. "And they're crazy. Did I mention that part already?"

The grin I'm trying to hide surfaces. "You did."

She frowns. "You want to spend a weekend on a farm in Wisconsin with a bunch of people you don't know who will interrogate you mercilessly?"

As long as I'm with her, I'll happily do anything. But if I tell her that, she'll freak out. So I give her the simple answer. "Yep. That's right. Glad you understand."

She searches my gaze, and I think she might turn me down, but then she gives a faint nod and holds out a hand. "Can I have my phone back?"

* * *

Enya

I'm tempted to take Jimmy up on his offer. It would save me a lot of awkwardness. I'm *very* tempted. But as he lays my phone on my palm, I don't immediately call Kelsey to let her know the news. Instead, I decide to give him one last chance to change his mind.

"It's sweet of you to offer, but I don't think you know what you're getting yourself into. You'll regret your decision about two-point-five seconds after you arrive, and by then it will be too late to escape."

He doesn't look away and gives no sign of reconsidering. "Whatever they throw at me, I can take it."

"You say that now."

"I won't flake out on you." He thrusts his chin forward, and everything about his stance screams of determination. I've got no idea why he's so dead set on this, but in this moment, I truly believe he means what he says.

I take a few seconds to appraise him. I've never thought of Jimmy as anything other than a training buddy. I make a point not to check out the guys I train with because it's easier to stay focused if I think of them as totally nonsexual entities. But I suppose I've known him for a few months now and never stopped to really see him.

He's lean, on the tall side of average, and has hooded blue eyes that seem to see right through me. They're unnerving. His dirty-blond hair is tied at the nape of his neck, and it's even longer than mine. He looks like any other fighter in his early twenties, except for the lack of tattoos. As far as I can tell, he has virgin skin, which makes him an oddity in our line of work. An oddity like me. It's not that I've never thought of getting a tattoo, but my sponsors like the girl-next-door look, and if I started getting ink, it would mess with that image. Considering they're responsible for a large portion of my livelihood, I go along with it. I won't be a fighter forever, and if I want tattoos down the track, it's never too late. Hell, my grandma just had a butterfly tattooed on her arm.

I cock my head. Jimmy is cute. He's also fun and dedicated to MMA. It's not beyond the realm of possibility that we'd be together. If I bring him along as my date, my family probably won't think anything of it. But then, there is that one thing....

"I'm too old for you," I tell him. He looks young for his age, which makes the difference even more obvious.

He lifts an eyebrow. "Are you nuts?"

"I'd like to think not, but with my family, who knows?"

He shakes his head in disbelief. "You're fucking gorgeous. Six years means nothing. You'd still be the most beautiful woman I know if you were six*teen* years older than me."

Something awakens in my stomach. A flutter of awareness. A flash of heat.

I shouldn't be flattered. Jimmy is the kind of guy

who talks a lot of shit. But he looks sincere. Does he actually think I'm beautiful? I mean, I know I'm pretty enough. If I wasn't, my sponsors wouldn't be so concerned about my image. But it's rare for a man to make a move on me. My theory is I intimidate non-fighters and just don't really click with fighters in a romantic sense.

"Well, thanks." I sound stilted and awkward, but I don't know how to take the compliment. I'm used to having my technique praised, but not my looks. And definitely not by a fit twenty-two-year-old with a heated gaze. "Are you really sure about this?"

"Yes." He steps forward. "Unless you'd rather go on five blind dates. If that's what you want, I'll leave right now. No problem."

"It's not." Especially not when I have a big fight coming up against the reigning British champion in my weight class. I need to focus all my attention on that. I've had many massive opportunities in the past few years, and I've always fallen short at the last hurdle. This is my chance to change that, and he's offering to help. The fluttering in my stomach morphs into a full-on tumble of nerves, but I find Kelsey's number in my phone and hit the Call button. "Hey, Kels. Sorry about cutting the call short."

"Oh my God!" she shrieks. "Who was that guy? He sounded hot. Is he hot?"

I exhale slowly and glance at Jimmy. "Yeah, he's hot."

His lips twist into a satisfied smirk that does ridiculous things to my insides.

"His name is Jimmy Parker. I've been seeing him for a little while now, and I didn't want to say anything because it's so new, but he's the reason I can't do any blind dates."

Kelsey squeals and I draw the phone away from my

ear before she deafens me. My baby sister doesn't have any volume control. "Are you bringing him? You'd better be. Because I want to meet him, and Mom will too."

And so would Emma, Maryanne, Pru, and Del. Within an hour, I'd no doubt hear from each of my siblings. They're an interfering crew. Normally, I love them for it, but sometimes they take it too far.

"Yes, I'm bringing him. So if you could tell everyone to cancel whatever blind dates they've set up, that would be great. Jimmy is a fighter, so I doubt anyone wants to go head-to-head with him."

"So hot," Kelsey whispers, and I can practically hear her fanning herself. "Consider them canceled. Please tell me he has good-looking friends."

I laugh at the thought of my exuberant sister fluttering her eyelashes at the guys from Crown MMA. Unfortunately for her, they don't generally mess with the family of their training buddies. "If you come to Vegas, I'd be happy to introduce you, but if you're hoping for a sexy new boyfriend, you might be out of luck."

"Such a killjoy," she mutters. "I'd better go help Maryanne with her homework. See you soon. I can't wait to meet your man."

I catch Jimmy's eye and smile. "Yeah, he can't wait to meet you either." We say goodbye, then Jimmy and I head toward our cars together. "You're in for it now," I tell him. "Just wait. Nothing can prepare you for an inquisition by the Sears girls."

He lifts a shoulder nonchalantly. "Bring it on."

ALSO BY A. RIVERS

Crown MMA Romance: The Outsiders

Fighter's Frenemy

Fighter's Fake Out

Fighter's Mercy

Fighter's Forever

Crown MMA Romance

Fighter's Heart

Fighter's Best Friend

Fighter's Secret

Fighter's Second Chance

King's Security

The King

The Veteran

ACKNOWLEDGMENTS

Thank you to everyone who helped bring this book to life. A massive thank you to my editors, Kate and Donna, and to Maria at Steamy Designs for the wonderful cover. Thank you to everyone who read this book—it's because of you that I get to do what I love. And most of all, a heartfelt thank you to my husband and family, who support me and don't mind when I have to disappear into the writing cave for a while. You're amazing.

ABOUT THE AUTHOR

Alexa (A.) Rivers writes romance with strong heroes and heroines who kick butt and take names. She loves MMA fighters, investigators, military men, bodyguards, and the protective guy next door who isn't afraid to fight the odds for love. She also writes small town romance as Alexa Rivers.